RESIDUALS:

COTYLORHYNCHUS RISES

Susan Smith Nash

Texture Press

RESIDUALS: COTYLORHYNCHUS RISES
Susan Smith Nash

Book 1 of the Residuals Series

Texture Press
1609 Oklahoma Avenue
Norman, OK 73071

Library of Congress CIP Data
Nash, Susan Smith, author.
Cotylorhynchus Rises / Susan Smith Nash.
pages cm. — (Residuals ; book 1)
ISBN 978-1-945784-21-7 (pbk.)

1. Fossils—Fiction. 2. Mental illness—Fiction. 3. Ghost
stories. 4. Oklahoma—Fiction. 5. Paleontology—Fiction. 6.
Quantum theory—Fiction. 7. Young adult fiction.
I. Title. II. Series: Residuals ; bk. 1.
PS3564.A77465 C68 2025
[Fic]—dc23
Young adult fiction; Oklahoma—Fiction
Description: In a YA paranormal sci-fi thriller, teens
investigate fossil beds and electromagnetic anomalies beneath
a haunted asylum, uncovering layers of trauma, intelligence,
and healing.
Cover design and interior layout by Susan Smith Nash.

Forays into an abandoned mental hospital in the shadows of a major university

Prehistoric extinction meets human trauma at Hope Hall, the abandoned asylum built atop fossil beds. Now, a girl with a physicist mother and a boy with a hacked magnetometer uncover that what died below never left.

Table of Contents

QUICK SYNOPSIS OF EPISODES:

EPISODE 1: POISONED PARADISE Kayla and her mother Dr. Garvin discuss the true nature of her quantum physics research at the Sam Noble Museum, revealing the connection between ancient Permian fossils and modern consciousness phenomena.

EPISODE 2: THE BURNING OF INNOCENCE Kayla and Epi encounter the spirits of 49 boys who died in the 1918 fire at Hope Hall, led by Billy Morrison, and help them find peace through acknowledgment and remembrance.

EPISODE 3: POSTPARTUM The team investigates the maternity ward and encounters Cora Gilstrap, a spirit from the 1918 era who experienced postpartum depression, learning about historical and modern approaches to maternal mental health.

EPISODE 4: WORKING WITH THE HORSES Exploring Hope Hall's equine therapy program through the spirits of James Wheeler (WWI veteran with shell shock) and his therapy horse Lightning, while connecting to modern therapeutic practices.

EPISODE 5: INVENTOR ON THE SPECTRUM The team helps Timothy Ashford, a young autistic inventor from the 1920s who was misunderstood and labeled as "possessed," while exploring historical and modern understanding of autism.

EPISODE 6: ANOREXIA AND THE FLAPPER AND THE FLYER Investigating eating disorders through the spirits of Margaret Worthington (suffragette who used hunger strikes) and Dorothy Fleming (1920s flapper with anorexia), connecting to modern cheerleader Jessica's struggles.

EPISODE 7: GLOVE MAN Encountering Theodore Whitman, who suffered from guilt-induced delusions about his hands after surviving an industrial accident, exploring themes of survivor's guilt and body dysmorphic disorder.

EPISODE 8: A BUBBLE AGAINST THE BULLIES Meeting Holly and her exploitative "protectors" Tommy and Frank in the hospital's vocational wing, while helping modern homeless teenager Zeno understand the difference between real protection and manipulation.

EPISODE 9: THE QUANTUM GHOST Dr. Garvin reveals her consciousness reconstruction research and warns of a collective entity forming at Hope Hall with the power to affect the physical world.

EPISODE 10: THE FRACTURE Mark struggles with doubt about Kayla's mental health versus supernatural abilities, while the collective entity makes contact with Epi, offering partnership in bridging living and dead consciousness.

EPISODE 11: THE WEIGHT OF TRUTH Epi confronts his own doubts about his autism and perceptions while the collective entity grows stronger and targets him specifically for his unique neurological patterns.

EPISODE 12: THE DISSOLUTION OF MINZIE Minzie encounters dark matter bushes that destabilize her physical form, causing her to experience multiple quantum states simultaneously before Kayla helps stabilize her consciousness.

EPISODE 13: THE MUSIC OF MEMORY Dr. Garvin's childhood memory of discovering consciousness as modular architecture through playing her grandmother's pump organ, leading to her development of mathematical proofs for consciousness reconstruction.

EPISODE 14: THE PRINCETON SHADOW Dr. Mikael Väisänen from Princeton begins monitoring and stealing the Norman team's research, while Dr. Sarah Kim infiltrates their operations under the guise of collaboration.

EPISODE 15: THE IVY LEAGUE DECEPTION Mark is manipulated by Dr. Kim into betraying the team by providing Princeton with documentation of their investigations, while Princeton's consciousness experiments fail catastrophically.

EPISODE 16: THE ACADEMIC THEFT Dr. Garvin discovers Princeton's systematic theft of her research while Princeton's team suffers from consciousness destabilization, developing an obsession with pickleball as their condition deteriorates.

EPISODE 17: EAST COAST VS. RED EARTH Direct confrontation between Princeton's military-grade consciousness control approach and the Norman team's ecological understanding, as reality begins fracturing under Princeton's crude interference.

EPISODE 18: THE OKLAHOMA CONVERGENCE The final battle between domination and participation approaches to consciousness research, with Kayla making contact with the quantum consciousness ocean and Princeton's team learning humility through failure.

PROLOGUE: THE WEIGHT OF ANCIENT EARTH

Long before Oklahoma existed as a name on any map, before the first human footsteps pressed into the red clay soil, the land that would become Norman was a vast, shallow sea teeming with life. During the Early Permian period, 290 million years ago, this ancient ocean supported one of Earth's most remarkable ecosystems—a world of massive synapsids that would vanish almost completely during the Great Dying that ended the Permian.

Among these creatures was *Cotylorhynchus romeri*, a massive herbivore that could grow to fifteen feet in length, making it one of the largest land animals of its time. Despite its impressive size, it was a gentle giant, feeding on the primitive plants that grew in the warm, humid climate of the Pangaean supercontinent. Its most distinctive feature was its enormously elongated body with an extraordinarily deep torso—almost barrel-shaped—that housed the massive digestive system needed to process large quantities of low-nutrition plant material. Unlike the sail-backed synapsids, *Cotylorhynchus* had a relatively low, rounded back profile that made it appear almost like a living table when viewed from the side.

When the Permian-Triassic extinction event struck 252 million years ago, these magnificent creatures were among the 96% of marine species and 70% of terrestrial vertebrates that perished in what scientists would later call the Great Dying. But death, as it turned out, was not the end of their story.

The *Cotylorhynchus* died where they lived—in the swamps and watering holes of what is now central Oklahoma. Their massive bodies sank into the mud and silt of the Hennessey Formation, where Lower Permian sediments would preserve them as some of the most complete synapsid fossils ever discovered. Layer by layer, millions of years of geological time buried them beneath what would eventually become the rolling hills of Norman, Oklahoma.

The irony was profound: the very ground that would later support one of the state's most prominent universities, and adjacent to it, one of its most troubled mental health institutions, rested atop one of the largest concentrations of *Cotylorhynchus romeri* fossils in North America. The Hennessey shale beneath Norman was a paleontological treasure trove, containing not just individual specimens but entire herds of these ancient creatures, their bones arranged in death assemblages that told the story of mass mortality events.

It was during the 1930s and 1940s that road construction workers building new streets throughout Norman began discovering peculiar bones embedded in the red Hennessey shale. The fossils were initially mistaken for cattle remains by the construction crews—an understandable error given the massive size of the bones and their relatively recent exposure. However, University of Oklahoma paleontologist J. Willis

Stovall and his colleagues would identify and extensively study them as belonging to *Cotylorhynchus romeri*. Stovall's groundbreaking work with these specimens would establish OU as a major center for vertebrate paleontology, leading to the creation of the Stovall Museum of Science and History, the university's first natural history museum, which housed the remarkable collection of synapsid fossils that Stovall and his crews excavated from the Norman area.

The timing of this discovery coincided with another significant development: the establishment of the Oklahoma Sanitarium Company and the construction of Central State Hospital. Just as the university was being built atop the fossil beds, plans were underway for a massive mental health facility that would house Oklahoma's most vulnerable citizens on the same ancient burial ground.

Central State Hospital: A City of the Troubled Mind

Construction began on Central State Hospital in 1895, just six years after the university's founding. The institution was initially called the Oklahoma Sanitarium, reflecting the era's optimistic belief that mental illness could be cured through proper treatment in the right environment. Dr. Griffin, the hospital's first president, envisioned a self-sufficient community that would provide both sanctuary and therapy for patients suffering from what were then broadly categorized as "nervous disorders," "hysteria," and "feeble-mindedness."

The hospital complex was ambitious in scope, designed to function as a small city. At its peak, Central State housed over 3,200 patients and employed more than 500 staff members. The campus included not just treatment facilities but also its own power plant, water treatment system, cannery, bakery, working farm, butchery, dairy, and laundry. Patients who were able participated in work therapy programs, tending crops, caring for livestock, and learning trades that might help them reintegrate into society.

The architectural style was deliberately imposing—Classical Revival buildings constructed from the same red brick and limestone that characterized the nearby university campus. This wasn't coincidental; both institutions were meant to project stability, permanence, and intellectual authority. The main building, later known as Hope Hall, featured towering arches, ornate stonework, and Corinthian columns that cast dramatic shadows across the meticulously maintained grounds.

But Central State's history was marked by both progressive innovations and tragic failures. The hospital pioneered several therapeutic approaches that were considered advanced for their time: occupational therapy, recreational activities, and what would now be called animal-assisted therapy using miniature horses and other farm animals. Many patients genuinely benefited from these programs, finding purpose and healing through structured activities and compassionate care.

However, the institution also reflected the prejudices and limitations of its era. Patients were often committed for behaviors that would be understood differently today—women for "hysteria" or refusing to obey their husbands, children for autism spectrum behaviors that were interpreted as "demonic possession," activists for political dissent that was labeled as "defiance disorder." The hospital's darker chapters included forced sterilizations, primitive shock treatments, and the tragic fire of April 13, 1918, that claimed the lives of 49 intellectually disabled boys who were locked in their dormitory when the flames spread.

The fire was particularly devastating because the hospital's wooden structures had been treated with paraffin for sanitary purposes—a practice that turned the buildings into tinderboxes when flames broke out. The boys who died were between ten and fifteen years old, sent to Central State by families who couldn't cope with their disabilities. When the fire began, staff evacuated themselves first, leaving the children trapped behind locked doors. The tragedy was quietly covered up to protect the hospital's reputation, and the victims were buried in unmarked graves.

As decades passed, Central State evolved with changing psychiatric practices. The name changed several times—from Oklahoma Sanitarium to Central State Hospital to Griffin Memorial Hospital—but the fundamental tension remained between therapeutic intentions and institutional control. The introduction of psychiatric medications in the 1950s transformed treatment approaches, but it also enabled widespread deinstitutionalization that often left vulnerable patients without adequate community support.

By the 1970s, the vast complex was largely abandoned. Griffin Memorial Hospital continued operating in a smaller capacity, but the grand Gothic buildings of the original Central State were left to decay. Nature began reclaiming the grounds, and stories of supernatural activity attracted urban explorers and paranormal investigators. Hope Hall, the iconic main building, became the focus of numerous ghost stories and legends.

The University Connection

The proximity of the University of Oklahoma to the former
Central State Hospital created an unusual dynamic. Less
than five miles separated the state's flagship university from
its largest mental health institution, yet the two existed in
parallel worlds that rarely intersected academically. OU
students would occasionally venture onto the abandoned
hospital grounds, but formal research connections were
limited.

This began to change in the early 21st century as university
researchers developed new interests in consciousness studies,
historical trauma, and the psychological impact of place-based
memory. The discovery that the Hennessey shale beneath
both institutions contained extraordinary concentrations of
Cotylorhynchus romeri fossils added another layer of
significance to the site.

The fossils weren't randomly distributed—geological surveys
revealed that the ancient creatures had died in specific
locations that corresponded to watering holes and gathering
places during the Permian period. These fossil concentrations
created what paleontologists called "death assemblages"—
sites where multiple organisms had perished simultaneously,
often during environmental crises or mass mortality events.

Dr. Alfred Sherwood Romer himself had studied the Norman
fossils extensively during the 1940s and 1950s, noting that
the preservation quality was exceptional and that the
concentration of specimens suggested the area had been a
crucial habitat for these ancient synapsids. The irony wasn't
lost on him that some of the finest *Cotylorhynchus* fossils
were being excavated from beneath a mental health

institution—as if the land itself held memories of both ancient death and modern suffering.

The Quantum Connection

What neither the university researchers nor the hospital administrators initially understood was that the geological formation beneath their institutions possessed unusual electromagnetic properties. The Hennessey shale, rich in iron compounds and crystalline structures, created natural piezoelectric effects that could store and amplify electromagnetic charges. This wasn't unique to Oklahoma—similar phenomena had been documented at other fossil-rich sites worldwide—but the combination of factors at Norman was particularly pronounced.

The presence of millions of fossilized organisms, each preserving the biochemical traces of ancient life, combined with the shale's electromagnetic properties to create what some researchers would later theorize was a form of "geological memory." The very rocks seemed to hold traces of the consciousness that had once existed there, layer upon layer of preserved experience stretching back through deep time.

Modern mental health facilities, with their abundance of extreme emotional states and psychological trauma, added contemporary layers to this ancient foundation. The Classical Revival buildings of Central State, constructed with iron frameworks and limestone facades, acted as inadvertent amplifiers for these electromagnetic effects. The result was an environment where the boundaries between past and present, between individual consciousness and collective memory, became permeable in ways that conventional science was only beginning to understand.

It would take a new generation of researchers—led by a quantum physicist masquerading as a paleontologist and her quantum-sensitive daughter—to begin unraveling the connections between ancient death, geological memory, and the persistent consciousness of those who had suffered within Hope Hall's Classical Revival walls.

The stage was set for discoveries that would challenge everything science thought it knew about consciousness, death, and the persistence of memory in the quantum foam that underlies all reality.

EPISODE 1: POISONED PARADISE

The late afternoon sun cast long shadows through the Modern windows of the Sam Noble Museum of Natural History as nineteen-year-old Kayla Garvin pressed her palm against the cool glass of the *Cotylorhynchus* display case. Today she wore one of her favorite combinations: a vintage Fleetwood Mac t-shirt layered under an oversized flannel shirt in deep purple, paired with jeans she'd hand-embroidered with tiny golden spirals around the cuffs. Her auburn hair was braided with thin silver threads that caught the light when she moved, and her mismatched earrings—a simple silver stud in her left ear and an intricate feather and bead creation in her right—clinked softly as she studied the massive skeleton.

The specimen before her was magnificent—fifteen feet of ancient bone arranged in a lifelike pose that captured the unique majesty of this Permian giant. The most striking feature was the creature's enormously elongated, barrel-shaped torso that dominated its low-slung profile, creating an almost table-like silhouette that spoke of its specialized adaptation for processing vast quantities of plant material. But it was the creature's relatively small skull that fascinated Kayla most—tiny in proportion to such a massive body, suggesting an intelligence different from but not necessarily inferior to modern mammals.

"Mom, what made you want to become a geologist?" she asked, watching dust motes dance in the golden light like microscopic spirits.

Dr. Shelley Garvin looked up from her research notes, her appearance a study in academic conservatism: pressed khaki pants, black long-sleeve knit shirt, simple gold stud earrings, and her thin gold chain necklace that held a small medallion engraved with Schrödinger's equation. Her uniform was deliberate camouflage in the university environment, designed to deflect attention from the radical nature of her actual research.

"T-Rex and all the other dinosaurs, of course," Dr. Garvin replied automatically, then paused as she caught her daughter's skeptical expression.

Kayla turned from the display case, her feather earring catching the museum's lighting. "Oh, Mom. I know that's not true! You're not a paleontologist—you work on other things."

Her mother smiled, recognizing the stubborn intelligence that Kayla had definitely inherited from her. "You're absolutely right, sweetheart. I should be honest with you." She set down her research folder. "I'm not a geologist or a paleontologist. I'm a quantum physicist."

"What?" Kayla's voice carried surprise and something else— relief, perhaps, that her mother was finally being truthful about the sophisticated equipment she'd been borrowing for her "ghost hunting" investigations.

"I study consciousness as a quantum phenomenon," Dr. Garvin continued, moving to join her daughter at the display. "The equipment I've been lending you doesn't detect fossils— it detects residual energy patterns left by conscious thought."

She gestured toward the *Cotylorhynchus* skeleton. "What we call 'history' might actually be the accumulated quantum signatures of every thought, emotion, and experience that's ever occurred in a location. When humans experience intense emotions—trauma, love, fear, revelation—those experiences leave quantum footprints in the local electromagnetic field."

Kayla adjusted the silver threads in her braid nervously. "You mean like... psychic imprints?"

"More like thought archaeology. The equipment you've been using can detect and analyze these quantum consciousness patterns." Dr. Garvin pulled out her tablet, showing complex waveform displays. "But Hope Hall is special, Kayla. The residual energy there is at least a hundred times stronger than anywhere else I've measured."

"Why?"

"Several factors converge there. First, the limestone foundation of the hospital buildings has piezoelectric properties—it can store and amplify electromagnetic charges. Second, the entire area sits on top of the Hennessey Formation."

Dr. Garvin opened a geological survey map on her tablet, showing the cross-section of rock layers beneath Norman. "The Hennessey shale is Lower Permian in age, about 290 million years old. But it's not just any Permian formation—it contains one of the highest concentrations of *Cotylorhynchus romeri* fossils in North America."

She pointed to areas marked in red on the geological map. "These zones indicate fossil concentrations. What you're looking at is essentially a mass graveyard from the end of the Permian period. Thousands, possibly millions of these creatures died in this specific area during the Great Dying 252 million years ago."

Kayla studied the map, noting how the fossil concentrations aligned perfectly with the current layout of Norman. "The university is built on top of them too."

"Exactly. But here's what makes it even more remarkable— the way they died. Most *Cotylorhynchus* fossils are found as isolated specimens, but in Norman, they're preserved in what paleontologists call 'death assemblages.' Entire herds that perished together, often in what appears to have been single catastrophic events."

Dr. Garvin opened another file showing fossil excavation photos from the 1940s and 1950s. "J. Willis Stovall documented several mass mortality sites during his extensive surveys of the Norman area. Groups of ten to twenty adult *Cotylorhynchus* found together, along with juveniles, suggesting these were family units or social groups that died simultaneously. The Stovall Museum became world-famous for housing some of the most complete specimens ever found."

"What killed them?"

"Probably a combination of factors related to the environmental changes that led to the Great Dying. Volcanic activity released massive amounts of carbon dioxide and sulfur compounds into the atmosphere. Ocean acidification, climate change, the collapse of food webs. These gentle giants depended on specific plant communities that began disappearing as the Permian period ended."

Kayla fingered the small dreamcatcher charm she'd woven into her braid—a gift from a Cherokee classmate who'd told her that some places held more memory than others. "So they experienced mass trauma before they died."

"Exactly. And that level of mass death—millions of conscious beings experiencing terror, pain, and loss simultaneously— created what I call a 'quantum trauma layer' in the geological substrate. The Hennessey shale literally absorbed and preserved the electromagnetic signatures of that ancient suffering."

Dr. Garvin's voice grew more excited as she continued her explanation. "But the story doesn't end there. When Central State Hospital was built directly on top of these fossil deposits, it created a unique situation. A mental health institution housing thousands of people in extreme psychological states, built on a foundation that was already saturated with ancient trauma energy."

She showed Kayla historical photos of Central State's construction in the 1890s, followed by images from the 1930s and 1940s road construction projects. "When they were building new roads throughout Norman in the 1930s and 1940s, workers kept finding these massive bones in the Hennessey shale. Road crew reports mention 'dragon bones' and some workers refusing to continue digging in certain areas, but the construction continued anyway."

"They knew about the fossils?"

"They knew something was unusual. J. Willis Stovall began his systematic study of the Norman specimens in the 1930s as more and more fossils were uncovered during the city's expansion. The irony wasn't lost on him—some of the most complete synapsid fossils ever discovered were coming from the same geological formation that supported both the university and the mental health facility. His work would eventually lead to the creation of the Stovall Museum, making OU famous worldwide for its Permian vertebrate collections."

Kayla adjusted her mismatched earrings, feeling the weight of this revelation. "So Hope Hall is built on top of an ancient mass grave."

"An ancient mass grave that's been amplified by a century of human psychological trauma, stored in piezoelectric limestone, and activated by modern electromagnetic fields." Dr. Garvin's expression grew serious. "Kayla, what you've been experiencing at Hope Hall isn't just individual spirits. You're interfacing with layered consciousness—Permian death events, historical human trauma, and something even more complex."

She pulled up recent quantum field readings from her monitoring equipment. "The electromagnetic signatures suggest that all this accumulated consciousness energy is beginning to organize itself into something collective. Something that might be aware of us studying it."

Kayla looked back at the *Cotylorhynchus* skeleton, seeing it with new understanding. The gentle curve of its neck, the massive body designed for a world of primitive plants and warm seas, the sad emptiness of the eye sockets that had once held ancient awareness—all of it suddenly felt personal, connected to her own experiences with the spirits at Hope Hall.

"The poor babies," she whispered, echoing what she'd said about the children who died in the fire. "They were just trying to survive in a changing world."

"And maybe," Dr. Garvin said softly, "that's exactly what the spirits at Hope Hall are trying to do too. Survive the transition from individual biological consciousness to something larger, more collective, more enduring."

She showed Kayla one final image—a quantum field map of Norman that looked remarkably like a neural network, with Hope Hall at its center and pathways of consciousness energy extending throughout the city along creek beds and limestone formations.

"The dark matter-concentrating plants you've been documenting aren't random vegetation, sweetheart. They're growing along the same geological formations that contain the highest fossil concentrations. It's as if the consciousness energy is using them to create its own nervous system."

Kayla studied the map, tracing the pathways with her finger. "A nervous system for what?"

"For something that might be the first truly post-biological intelligence—a merger of ancient consciousness, human awareness, and quantum information processing. The question is: are we witnessing the birth of a new form of life, or are we being recruited to become part of something that's been waiting millions of years to fully awaken?"

As they prepared to leave the museum, Kayla pressed her palm against the display case one final time. For just a moment, she could swear she felt a pulse of warmth from the ancient bones, as if some trace of the creature's consciousness still lingered in the fossilized calcium phosphate.

"Tell them we weren't bad," she whispered, remembering Billy Morrison's final words. "Tell them we were just trying to survive."

Dr. Garvin heard her daughter's words and felt a chill of recognition. The same plea—for understanding, for remembrance, for dignity in death—connected the ancient synapsids, the forgotten patients of Hope Hall, and perhaps every conscious being that had ever faced extinction.

Outside the museum, the late afternoon sun painted the University of Oklahoma campus in golden light, its red brick buildings echoing the Classical Revival architecture of Hope Hall just a few miles away. Beneath their feet, the Hennessey shale held its ancient secrets, and somewhere in the quantum foam between past and present, both *Cotylorhynchus* and human spirits waited for someone to finally understand that all consciousness—ancient and modern, individual and collective—deserved to be honored rather than exploited.

The stage was set for investigations that would challenge everything they thought they knew about life, death, and the persistence of awareness across the vast spans of geological time.

EPISODE 2: THE BURNING OF INNOCENCE

The boarded window of Hope Hall swiveled mysteriously when Epi touched it, opening just wide enough for him and Kayla to slip through. The evening shadows were deepening across the abandoned grounds, and the Classical Revival architecture looked even more imposing in the twilight. The massive Corinthian columns cast long shadows across the overgrown courtyard, their clean lines and formal proportions creating a stark contrast to the Prairie Classical Revival gargoyles that watched over the university campus just miles away.

"I can't believe this thing just... opens," Kayla whispered, glancing back at the window that had closed behind them.

"The Backpack Mag is already picking up anomalous readings," Epi said, adjusting the settings on his device. The rutilated quartz crystals caught the last rays of sunlight filtering through broken windows. "There's definitely some kind of magnetic field disturbance in this place, but the patterns are unlike anything in the baseline geological surveys."

They found themselves in what had once been a reception area. Faded murals still decorated the walls—scenes of peaceful gardens and smiling faces that now looked grotesque in the dim light. Their footsteps echoed on cracked marble floors as they moved deeper into the building.

"According to my research," Epi said, consulting his phone while monitoring the real-time data streaming to his cloud-based analysis app, "the worst tragedy happened in the children's wing. April 13, 1918. Forty-nine boys died in a fire."

Kayla shivered. "Intellectually disabled kids, right? Sent here because their families couldn't cope."

"Or were ashamed," Epi added grimly. "Back then, having a 'defective' child was considered a family disgrace. These boys were between ten and fifteen years old."

The Backpack Magnetometer began registering faster fluctuations in the Earth's magnetic field as they approached a corridor marked with a faded sign: "CHILDREN'S WARD - BOYS." The walls here showed fire damage that had never been fully repaired—blackened stone and twisted metal fixtures that looked like skeletal remains.

"Epi, your machine is detecting major magnetic field variations."

"The readings are off the charts. Whatever happened here left a massive electromagnetic signature." He adjusted several parameters on his device, and the data visualization on his connected tablet showed rapid spikes in magnetic field intensity. "Kayla, I think we're picking up residual magnetic disturbances from the iron in the building's infrastructure—metal bed frames, plumbing, electrical conduits that were superheated during the fire and may have retained unusual magnetic properties."

A child's voice cut through the darkness: "Help us! Please, somebody help us!"

They froze. The voice seemed to come from everywhere and nowhere, echoing off the damaged walls with increasing desperation.

"Fire! FIRE! The stairs are burning!"

More voices joined the first—dozens of young voices crying out in terror and confusion. The temperature in the corridor dropped noticeably, and their breath began misting in the suddenly frigid air. Epi's magnetometer showed massive spikes in magnetic field variations, as if the very air around them was being disturbed by some invisible force.

"We can't get out! The doors are locked!"

Kayla's heart clenched at the panic in those young voices. "The poor babies," she whispered. "They were trapped."

Through the broken windows, an orange glow began to flicker—not from any real fire, but from some kind of electromagnetic phenomenon that Epi's equipment was struggling to categorize. The smell of smoke filled the air, mixed with something even more heartbreaking: the scent of paraffin that had been used to waterproof the wooden walls and stairs.

"The paraffin," Epi said, his voice tight with horror as he reviewed historical building records on his tablet. "They soaked the wood in paraffin for sanitary reasons. When the fire started..."

"It turned the whole building into a death trap," Kayla finished.

The ghostly voices grew more desperate: "Why won't anyone come? Where are the nurses? Where are the doctors?"

A small figure materialized at the end of the corridor—a boy of perhaps twelve, wearing the simple institutional clothing of the era. His face was streaked with soot, and his eyes held a terror that death hadn't erased.

"Miss, can you help us?" he asked, his voice barely a whisper. "We've been waiting so long for someone to come. We've been waiting for someone to remember us."

Kayla stepped forward, tears streaming down her face. "What's your name, sweetheart?"

"Billy Morrison. I'm from Tulsa. My mama sent me here because I can't read good, and I get confused sometimes. But I'm not bad! I try to be good!"

More ghostly figures began appearing—dozens of boys ranging from ten to fifteen, all wearing the same institutional uniforms, all bearing the marks of their terrifying final moments. Epi's magnetometer was clicking so rapidly it sounded like digital rainfall, and his real-time analysis app was creating 3D visualizations of magnetic field disturbances that seemed to cluster around each apparition.

"We didn't understand why no one came," Billy continued. "The smoke got so thick, and the stairs collapsed. We huddled together in the dormitory, but the fire found us anyway."

"The staff abandoned you," Kayla said, her voice breaking. "When the fire started, they saved themselves and left you locked in."

"We know that now," said another boy, older than Billy. "But for the longest time, we thought we'd done something wrong. We thought maybe we deserved it because we were different."

Epi's device was recording massive electromagnetic anomalies throughout the corridor. "Kayla, the magnetic field readings suggest these aren't just visual phenomena. There are actual disturbances in the local electromagnetic environment— changes in magnetic field intensity that correspond to each figure's location."

"What are you waiting for?" Kayla asked gently.

Billy stepped closer, his ghostly form somehow registering as a distinct magnetic signature on Epi's equipment. "We want people to know what really happened. We want them to know we were here. We want them to know we mattered."

"No one's supposed to remember the boys who died," added another spirit. "It was bad for the hospital's reputation. They buried us in unmarked graves and never talked about us again."

"But you do matter," Kayla said firmly. "You all matter. And people will remember you. I promise."

The ghostly figures seemed to glow brighter at her words, and Epi's magnetometer registered a shift in the electromagnetic patterns—from chaotic disturbance to something more harmonious and stable. Billy smiled—the first peaceful expression Kayla had seen on any of their faces.

"Thank you, miss. We've been so lonely."

One by one, the spirits began to fade, but not with the violence of being banished. Instead, they seemed to dissolve gently, like morning mist touched by sunlight. As they disappeared, Epi's magnetic field readings gradually returned to normal baseline levels. Billy was the last to go.

"Tell them we weren't bad," he said. "Tell them we were just little boys who needed help."

As the last spirit vanished, the temperature returned to normal, and the phantom smell of smoke dissipated. Epi's device settled into gentle, regular magnetic field variations that suggested the electromagnetic disturbances had somehow resolved themselves.

"They're at peace now," he said wonderingly, studying the data on his tablet. "The magnetic field signature has completely changed. It's stable now. Peaceful."

Kayla wiped her eyes and pulled out her phone. "I'm calling the Norman Historical Society first thing tomorrow. And the newspaper. And anyone else who will listen. Those boys are going to be remembered properly."

As they prepared to leave through the mysteriously swiveling window, Kayla looked back at the children's wing one last time. For just a moment, she could have sworn she saw Billy Morrison waving goodbye from one of the broken windows, finally free to rest after more than a century of waiting for someone to care.

Outside, a family of opossums emerged from the underbrush—not the strange, poisoned creatures that would later haunt Imhoff Creek, but healthy animals that seemed to nod respectfully toward the building before disappearing into the night.

The limestone foundations of Hope Hall settled with an almost audible sigh, and Epi's magnetometer registered one final, gentle fluctuation in the Earth's magnetic field—as if the building itself was finally able to rest.

EPISODE 3: POSTPARTUM

"Mom, did you have postpartum depression after you had me?" Kayla asked as they sat in Dr. Garvin's kitchen, sharing morning coffee before her mother left for the university.

Dr. Garvin paused with her mug halfway to her lips. "No. Not that I remember. But maybe a little bit. I was very anxious and I ate to calm my nerves. I gained twenty pounds after you were born. I dropped it immediately after you started walking—running! Chasing after you."

"That's funny, but it's a serious thing. Mark's cousin had a baby three months ago and he said the family is really worried about her."

"What are they doing for her?"

"Nothing. Mark said it's really hard to see a doctor and she doesn't have very good insurance, so they're going through all the paperwork."

Dr. Garvin set down her coffee. "I would imagine they'll give her meds. That can work."

"If they take them. I'm worried."

"They used to treat postpartum depression differently."

"Rest cure? Forced bed rest by your husband until you totally snap, 'Yellow Wallpaper' style?"

"No, but close. Maybe we can learn something from the past. I don't know. We don't seem to be doing much to help new mothers."

Kayla leaned forward. "Mark said his cousin needs real help. He's afraid she'll hurt herself or the baby."

That afternoon, Kayla found Epi in the university's engineering lab, tinkering with his Backpack Magnetometer. "Hey, Epi. You know that device you're working on—do you think it could help us find the wing at Central State where they committed new moms who tried to hurt themselves or their babies?"

Epi looked up from a tangle of wires and crystal arrays. "It's possible. We'll have to do research on the kinds of treatment they gave them, and the facilities—then perhaps we can do a 3D simulation and also replicate the types of metals—see if there is any vestigial energy."

Mark appeared in the doorway, looking skeptical. "I'm having a hard time believing this. We need to find out what they did in the past and if it worked."

"I'm just hoping it wasn't pure shock treatment and lobotomies," Kayla said.

"You know, at the time, it was considered progressive, not cruel," Epi pointed out.

Mark crossed his arms. "What's crueler? That, or doing nothing—until the poor woman snaps, hurts herself and her baby?"

"Sometimes I think we're all doomed here on Planet Earth," Kayla muttered.

"We are. But what the heck," Epi grinned, shouldering his equipment.

Later that night, they crept through the shadows toward Hope Hall. The winter landscape offered no cover—no shrubs or scrubby trees to block their lights from any security patrols.

"I hate it during the winter," Kayla whispered as they approached the mysteriously unlocked entrance.

"Here's the door," Mark said, pushing it open with surprising ease.

"What's that? Did you hear it? A clicking," Kayla asked, freezing.

"Don't be so jumpy! That was me. I just turned on my Backpack Mag. It's sending out signals and it should be letting us know when we have an anomaly," Epi explained.

"What kind?" Mark asked.

"I did research and have the patterns and overall profile of a women's ward for new mothers. In my research, I found it had a few items that made it unique and unlike other parts of the hospital."

"Like what?"

"Metal rocking chairs. Metal cribs. Rubber baby dolls."

Kayla stopped dead. "Cribs? To endanger the babies?"

"Quiet! I'm getting something," Epi hissed.

They crept down a dark hallway in complete silence except for the light clicking of the Backpack Mag. The Classical Revival architecture seemed to press in around them, creating shadows that moved independently of their flashlight beams.

"The Backpack Mag is sending out very strong signals," Epi whispered. "It's supposed to detect the anomalies. At the same time, though, I'm afraid it might stir something up."

"What? Stir something up?" Kayla asked, alarmed.

"Now you tell us! Like what?" Mark demanded.

"Energy. The vibrations can potentially 'awaken' something. I'm not saying it will. But hypothetically it can."

"Hush! Be quiet! I hear something!" Kayla grabbed both their arms.

Rhythmic grating sounds and very low moaning echoed from deeper in the building. The sounds seemed to pulse with a biological rhythm—like breathing, or rocking.

"It's coming from that hallway!" Mark pointed toward a corridor they hadn't explored before.

They made their way down the hallway and turned into a shorter corridor where the noise was loudest. At the end, they found two double doors.

"I'm sure they're locked. Let's go," Kayla said, already turning to leave.

"Wait! Look!" Epi pointed at the doors with excitement.

Mark shone his flashlight on them. "Wow! Do you see that? The doors look like they're glowing!"

"The Backpack Mag is detecting something for sure. The doors are shaking!" Epi's device was clicking frantically now.

"Oh no!" Kayla backed away as the doors began to emit a greenish glow, then suddenly stopped shaking. The two doors started to creak open slowly, seemingly of their own accord.

"I'm out of here! This is scary!" Kayla turned to run.

"Epi, I think your machine is working," Mark said grimly. "Kayla—we've got to give it a shot. My cousin might die or hurt her baby if she doesn't get some sort of help now."

Epi took a deep breath. "I'm opening the door. Get your flashlights ready."

They stepped through the doorway into what had once been the maternity ward. The smell of baby powder and baby shampoo was overwhelming, mixed with the institutional odors of carbolic acid and starch. In the center of the room sat a metal rocking chair, moving back and forth with no visible occupant.

Then, gradually, a woman materialized in the chair. She was holding a crocheted baby blanket in her arms, rocking back and forth with mechanical precision. Her form wavered like a hologram, occasionally becoming transparent.

"You can't wait. Do nothing and it will be too late," she said, her voice echoing strangely. "You can't wait. Do nothing and it will be too late."

Mark stepped forward cautiously. "Why are you here? What happened?"

"What's your name?" Kayla added gently.

The ghostly woman looked up at them with eyes full of ancient pain. "I'm Cora Gilstrap. This is my story. I was a teacher in Oklahoma City. My husband was an accountant. I stopped teaching after my baby was born. My husband died during the flu season in 1918. My baby would not stop crying. I started doing things to make the baby sick so that I'd have to take it to the doctor and so someone would help me out at home. But my sister-in-law found out I was making the baby sick so I could get help and then be lauded for nursing the baby back to health. My sister wanted me to go to prison. Instead, they sent me to Hope Hall. The baby is with my sister-in-law. After I was here for a few months, they were able to visit every Sunday."

"What are they doing for you?" Kayla asked.

"Lobotomy?" Mark whispered, horrified.

"Mark!" Kayla scolded.

Cora smiled, the first peaceful expression they'd seen on her face. "I'm in a group. The Scientific Ways of Motherhood."

"Is it working?" Kayla asked hopefully.

"Yes. It's all about having a system and checking off the things to do each day. Also, you can't be alone. The checklist includes things I do for the family as well as my baby. It is important to live with your family."

"Even if you don't have a family?" Epi asked.

"Everyone has some sort of family. You just have to learn how to make peace."

"And expand the definition of 'family,' I think," Epi nodded.

"But did you try to hurt yourself?" Kayla asked gently.

"Oh, yes."

"Even here?"

"Oh, yes."

"Did you eventually get better?"

Cora's face lit up with genuine joy. "My daughter grew up, got married, and started a flower shop."

"So things worked out," Kayla said, relieved.

"Oh, yes."

As Cora spoke those words, her peaceful expression suddenly twisted into something terrifying. She rocketed out of the chair, brandishing a massive surgical knife and lunging at Kayla with murderous intent.

Kayla fell backward, tripping over debris, while Epi frantically adjusted dials on the Backpack Mag. The clicking increased in volume and tempo, sounding like castanets. The metal rocking chair began glowing red-hot, radiating waves of heat that made the air shimmer.

Cora vanished as suddenly as she had appeared.

A small booklet skittered across the floor toward them. Mark snatched it up as they ran from the room, down the hallways, the castanets clattering behind them.

Once outside, they ran to Mark's Jeep and drove away from the Classical Revival pillars of the abandoned asylum as fast as safely possible. They didn't stop until they reached the Braum's Ice Cream restaurant, where they huddled in a booth, still shaking.

"Let's see what she left us," Mark said, opening the booklet. "'The New Mother's Handbook: A Checklist of Love.'"

"I'm still shaking," Kayla admitted.

"I wonder if anything Cora said could help my cousin," Mark mused.

"I think I'm going to start crying," Kayla said.

"Hang in there. You'll be okay," Mark assured her.

Epi was already studying his device's readouts. "The magnetometer did some very strange things, and I can't wait to plug it into the computer and download the sensor data. She wasn't really giving the reading of a person, you know."

"Well, duh! She was a ghost," Kayla said.

"I don't know. It was not an image only or electromagnetic energy. There was more to it than that."

"They've called our number," Mark said, pointing to the counter.

"I'm never doing this again," Kayla declared.

As she said that, a couple walked past their booth—a young woman in a hoodie carrying a baby, accompanied by a man in a khaki hunting coat. The young woman had dark brown hair and small gold earrings. As she passed their table, she looked directly at Kayla, pressed her lips together in a thin line, and clearly mouthed the words: "Thank you."

Mark and Epi returned with trays of food and drinks, but Kayla couldn't stop thinking about that young mother's grateful expression. Maybe their terrifying encounter with Cora's spirit had somehow helped—maybe the message about not waiting, about getting help immediately, had reached someone who needed to hear it.

Outside the restaurant window, a red fox trotted across the parking lot, pausing to look back at them through the glass. Its eyes held the same intelligence they'd noticed before, as if it were keeping watch over their supernatural investigations.

EPISODE 4: WORKING WITH THE HORSES

The miniature horses at Flames to Hope Ranch moved with gentle precision around the veterans in the equine therapy circle. Kayla watched from what she considered a safe distance—at least twenty feet back from the nearest horse—as a young man barely older than herself tentatively reached out to stroke the mane of a particularly patient mare named Daisy.

Unlike the stocky, sometimes stubborn Shetland ponies that most people were familiar with, these miniature horses were proportioned like full-sized horses, just scaled down. Daisy stood barely thirty inches tall at her withers, her coat a rich chestnut that gleamed in the afternoon sun. Her head was refined and delicate, with large, intelligent dark eyes that seemed to see directly into people's souls. Her mane fell in silky waves, and despite her small stature, she moved with the same elegant gait as her full-sized cousins.

"These horses are incredible," Kayla murmured to Epi, who was documenting the session for his latest research project, though her voice carried an edge of tension. "They seem to know exactly what each person needs."

What Kayla didn't say was that horses had always terrified her. Full-sized horses were massive, unpredictable creatures that had spent her childhood trying to scrape her off on low-hanging branches, or simply deciding mid-ride that they'd rather return to the barn than continue on the trail. Even these miniature versions made her nervous, though she couldn't quite articulate why something the size of a large dog should inspire the same visceral fear.

Mark nodded from where he stood with Minzie, both of them volunteering as session assistants. "The therapist said some of these guys haven't spoken in months. But something about the horses..."

"Animals don't judge," Dr. Garvin observed. She had joined them today, explaining that Hope Hall had once operated a similar program during its heyday. "But horses are particularly sensitive to human emotion in ways that even dogs and cats aren't. They're prey animals—their survival has always depended on reading the emotional states of everything around them. A horse can detect your heart rate from across a paddock."

The young veteran—his name tag read "Tommy"—was now sitting cross-legged next to Daisy. The miniature horse had positioned herself so that her body formed a protective barrier between Tommy and the rest of the group, creating a sense of privacy and safety. Her ears were swiveled toward him, and her breathing had synchronized with his—a phenomenon that therapists called "co-regulation."

"What's remarkable," continued the head therapist, a woman named Sarah who'd worked with both full-sized and miniature horses, "is that horses mirror our emotional states back to us instantly. If you're anxious, they become anxious. If you're calm, they calm down. It forces people to become aware of their own internal state in a way that other therapies can't."

Tommy was now whispering something they couldn't hear. Daisy had lowered her head to his level, breathing gently near his face. Her nostrils flared softly as she took in his scent, processing the chemical signals of his emotional state. When he raised his hand tentatively toward her neck, she remained perfectly still, allowing the contact.

"Dr. Garvin," Epi said, adjusting his small recording device, "do you think the energy signatures from therapeutic encounters like this could leave residual imprints? I mean, if healing energy is as real as traumatic energy..."

"You're thinking about Hope Hall again," Dr. Garvin said with a knowing smile. "What did you find in the children's wing?"

Kayla exchanged glances with her friends. They hadn't told her mother about their success with Billy Morrison and the other boys' spirits, or about their terrifying encounter with Cora Gilstrap.

"We found evidence that some of the therapeutic programs really worked," Kayla said carefully. "Maybe not all of the hospital's reputation was deserved."

Dr. Garvin nodded thoughtfully. "Actually, equine therapy has a longer history in mental health treatment than most people realize. As early as the 1860s, institutions in Europe were using horses to help patients with various psychiatric conditions. The theory was that caring for another living being—something dependent on you—could restore a sense of purpose and self-worth."

She gestured toward the miniature horses. "Hope Hall was actually progressive in their use of smaller horses. Full-sized horses can be intimidating, especially for patients who were already dealing with trauma. Miniature horses provide the same therapeutic benefits but in a less overwhelming package."

Kayla watched as another miniature horse—a black pinto named Patches who stood barely twenty-eight inches tall—approached a veteran in a wheelchair. The horse's coat was a patchwork of black and white, and his intelligent eyes were framed by a forelock that fell between them like a curtain. Despite his small size, he moved with the same noble bearing as a full-sized stallion.

"The rescue aspect is important too," Sarah added, overhearing their conversation. "Many of our therapy horses are rescues. Horses are expensive to maintain—food, veterinary care, farrier work—and during economic downturns, many owners simply abandon them. We've had horses come to us who were skin and bones, covered in rain rot, with hooves so overgrown they could barely walk."

Kayla's chest tightened at the description. Something about the idea of abandoned animals—creatures left to fend for themselves—made her feel physically sick.

"The rehabilitation process works both ways," Sarah continued. "Our clients help care for the rescued horses, nursing them back to health. There's something profoundly healing about saving something that was discarded, especially for people who feel discarded themselves."

She pointed to a teenage girl who was brushing a small gray mare named Hope. "That's Liliana—she's been in and out of foster care since she was eight. When Hope came to us, she'd been abandoned in a field for months. Liliana has spent every day for the past six months working with her, and now Hope is one of our best therapy horses."

Kayla felt her heart rate spike. The casual mention of foster care, of abandonment, of children moving from home to home hit something deep inside her. She pressed her hand to her chest, trying to steady her breathing, and immediately noticed Epi's magnetometer giving off an unusual reading— not the frantic clicking they associated with ghostly manifestations, but a low, complex hum that seemed to layer different frequencies on top of each other.

"Are you okay?" Minzie asked, noticing Kayla's sudden pallor.

"Fine," Kayla said quickly, pushing down whatever had just surfaced. "Just... horses make me nervous."

But it wasn't just the horses. The story about Liliana triggered something she didn't want to examine—memories that felt too close to the surface, too dangerous to acknowledge.

That evening, armed with this new perspective, they returned to Hope Hall. The boarded window swiveled open as always, admitting them to the increasingly familiar corridors. This time, they sought out the areas that had once housed the hospital's farm and therapy programs.

"According to the blueprints I found," Epi said, consulting his tablet, "the horse stables were connected to the main building through this wing. They had miniature horses specifically for therapy—just like Flames to Hope."

The Backpack Magnetometer was already giving off readings, but they were different from the traumatic energy signatures they'd encountered before. This felt warmer, more complex.

They moved through a series of rooms that showed evidence of having been converted from patient quarters to something more open and airy. Large windows, now broken and overgrown with vines, would have provided natural light and fresh air. The floors showed wear patterns consistent with regular foot traffic—not the shuffling gait of heavily medicated patients, but purposeful movement.

"This feels different," Kayla observed, though she stayed closer to the walls, away from the center of the space where horses would have been led through. "The energy here isn't dark like the other places we've explored."

They emerged into what had once been an indoor therapy arena. Though the roof had partially collapsed and vegetation had begun reclaiming the space, the basic structure remained. At the far end, they could make out the remains of small stalls—perfectly sized for miniature horses. Feed bins, built low to the ground, were still bolted to the walls.

"Hello? Is anyone here?" Kayla called softly, though she remained near the entrance.

A gentle nickering sound echoed through the space, though they could see no animals. The temperature rose slightly, and the air filled with the warm, comforting scent of hay and horses—that distinctive smell of sweet grain, leather, and the musky comfort of animal presence.

From the shadows emerged a young man in a World War I uniform, leading a ghostly miniature horse. Unlike the traumatized spirits they'd encountered before, this soldier walked with purpose and calm. The horse beside him was a stunning bay, perhaps thirty-two inches tall, with a black mane and tail that flowed like silk. His coat held the rich, warm brown of chestnuts in autumn, and his eyes were large and kind.

"You're here about the horses," the soldier said, his voice carrying a slight Southern accent. "I'm Private First Class James Wheeler. From Tennessee. They sent me here after..." He gestured vaguely toward his head. "After the shells got too loud in my mind."

"Shell shock," Epi said quietly. "What we'd call PTSD now."

James nodded. "The doctors here, they tried all sorts of things. Some worked, some didn't. But when they brought me to work with Lightning here"—he patted the miniature horse's neck—"that's when the noise started to quiet down."

Lightning was clearly a therapy horse, even in death. His posture was alert but calm, his ears pricked forward with interest rather than alarm. Despite being a spirit, he radiated the same peaceful energy they'd observed at Flames to Hope.

"Lightning was a therapy horse?" Kayla asked, staying carefully back from the ghostly pair.

"Best there ever was. He had this way of knowing when the memories were coming back. He'd step closer, put his head against my chest, and somehow... somehow the weight of him would anchor me to the present moment."

James noticed Kayla's distance and smiled gently. "You're afraid of horses."

"They're unpredictable," Kayla said defensively. "Even the little ones."

"That's exactly why they're perfect for therapy," James said. "Horses don't lie. They can't pretend to be something they're not. If you're scared, they know it. If you're angry, they feel it. If you're hiding something, they sense that too."

The ghostly horse nickered again and took a step toward them. To their amazement, they could feel warmth radiating from his form. Kayla instinctively stepped back.

"Lightning won't hurt you," James said. "But he knows you're carrying something heavy. Horses have this way of sensing pain, even when we try to hide it."

"Why are you still here?" Mark asked gently, perhaps sensing Kayla's discomfort.

James smiled, an expression of genuine peace. "I'm not stuck here like some of the others. Lightning and I, we chose to stay. There are still soldiers out there who need what we learned. When young people like yourselves come looking for answers, we want to help."

"What did you learn?" Kayla asked, though she kept her distance.

"That healing isn't about forgetting the bad things. It's about finding something stronger than the fear. For me, that was the connection with Lightning. The responsibility of caring for him gave me a reason to stay present, stay grounded."

James led them to one of the old stalls, where ghostly tack still hung on ethereal hooks. The space was designed for miniature horses—everything scaled down appropriately. Feed buckets hung at the perfect height for thirty-inch horses, and the stall doors were built lower than those for full-sized horses.

"We worked together every day for three years. I learned to groom him, feed him, exercise him. But more than that, I learned to trust again. To be trusted."

"The veterans at Flames to Hope," Minzie said suddenly. "They're learning the same thing."

"Exactly. The horses don't care about your nightmares or your scars. They only care about how you treat them in this moment. That teaches you to live in this moment too."

Lightning moved closer to Kayla, who had remained silent throughout the encounter. The miniature horse lowered his head and breathed gently near her face—the same gesture they'd witnessed at the ranch. Despite her fear, she found herself frozen in place as the ghost horse studied her with those impossibly kind eyes.

"He remembers," James said softly. "Lightning recognizes the same pain we used to carry. He's telling you that healing is possible."

"I'm not..." Kayla started, then stopped. Lightning was looking at her with the same expression she'd seen Daisy give Tommy—complete acceptance, no judgment, just acknowledgment of pain.

"The thing about horses," James continued, "is that they've often been abandoned too. Cast off when they're no longer useful, left to starve when times get hard. Lightning came to us as a rescue. Someone had turned him loose in the mountains when they couldn't afford to feed him anymore."

Kayla's breathing became shallow. The magnetometer in Epi's pack was producing that complex humming sound again, frequencies layering and interfering with each other.

"But here's what Lightning taught me," James said, his voice gentle. "Being abandoned doesn't make you worthless. Sometimes it just means you haven't found your real purpose yet."

Lightning stepped even closer to Kayla, close enough that she could feel his ghostly breath on her hands. Instead of the panic she expected, she felt something else—a recognition, as if this small horse understood something about her that she wasn't ready to understand about herself.

The Backpack Magnetometer's readings had been steady throughout most of the encounter—not the frantic clicking of traumatic energy, but a warm, consistent tone. But now, with Lightning so close to Kayla, the readings were becoming more complex, multiple emotional frequencies seeming to resonate together.

"You don't need our help to rest in peace," Epi observed, though he was watching his equipment with concern.

"No, we're quite peaceful already. But we stay to help others find their way to the same peace. Every person who learns to heal breaks the cycle a little more."

Lightning nickered softly and touched his nose to Kayla's hand. For just a moment, she felt a flash of understanding—not of her own pain, but of his. The memory of being hungry, alone, abandoned. And then the memory of being found, cared for, given purpose.

"He wants you to know," James said quietly, "that sometimes the things that hurt us the most are also the things that make us able to help others."

As they prepared to leave, James offered one final piece of wisdom: "Tell the young veterans that the horses will teach them what we learned—that courage isn't the absence of fear. It's feeling the fear and choosing to care for something else anyway."

Lightning nickered a gentle farewell as the spirits faded, not vanishing in distress but simply becoming transparent until they were no longer visible.

Outside Hope Hall, they found a real miniature horse waiting for them—a mare that looked remarkably similar to Daisy from the ranch. She stood calmly beside their car, her coat a rich chestnut that gleamed in the moonlight. At barely twenty-nine inches tall, she was perfectly proportioned like a full-sized horse, with delicate legs and an elegant neck. Her mane fell in gentle waves, and her large, dark eyes held the same intelligent kindness they'd seen in Lightning.

"Where did she come from?" Mark asked, bewildered.

Kayla approached the horse slowly, remembering James's lessons about trust and presence. The mare allowed herself to be petted, her coat warm and real under Kayla's trembling fingers. For a moment, Kayla felt the same peace she'd experienced with Lightning's ghost—a sense that this small creature understood something important about survival, about being found when you thought you were lost forever.

The mare whickered softly, then turned and trotted away toward the direction of Flames to Hope Ranch, her hooves making a gentle rhythmic sound on the asphalt.

"I think Lightning sent her," Kayla said softly, watching the horse disappear into the night. "To let us know the healing continues."

But as they drove away, Kayla found herself thinking not about Lightning or the visiting mare, but about the stories of abandonment—horses left to starve, children moved from home to home, the way people could simply disappear from each other's lives. The magnetometer continued its complex humming in the back seat, as if it were picking up on emotional frequencies that were still unresolved, still seeking their own form of healing.

EPISODE 5: INVENTOR ON THE SPECTRUM

"Help me, please help me!" The voice echoed through the night air around Hope Hall, tinny and repetitive, like a broken recording playing on an endless loop. "Help me, please help me!"

Kayla, Epi, and Mark had been investigating the hospital's records building when the cry pierced the darkness. They rushed toward the sound, following it through the Classical Revival corridors until they reached what had once been the children's educational wing.

"There!" Minzie pointed toward a window on the second floor, where a shadowy figure appeared briefly before vanishing. "Did you see him?"

The boy materialized again for just a moment—thin, maybe thirteen years old, with wild hair and eyes that held a desperate intelligence. Then he was gone, leaving only the echoing plea: "Help me, please help me!"

"He's stuck in a loop," Epi observed, his Backpack Magnetometer clicking frantically. The sound triggered something in him—a memory of his own repetitive behaviors, the way he'd rock back and forth when overwhelmed, until classmates learned to exploit it. "Something traumatic happened here, and he can't break free from that moment."

Car headlights swept across the building's facade—a security patrol. They ducked behind a crumbling wall as the vehicle passed, then waited until the sound of the engine faded before emerging.

"We have to come back," Kayla whispered. "That boy needs help."

The next day, Kayla spent hours in the university library researching autism and its historical understanding. What she found made her stomach turn. In the early 20th century, children with autism spectrum disorders were often misdiagnosed as "possessed," "feeble-minded," or suffering from "dementia praecox."

"Look at this," she told Epi, showing him a medical journal from 1925. "They called it 'demonic possession' when kids couldn't make eye contact or had repetitive behaviors. Some families actually tried exorcisms. And here—" She pointed to another article. "They classified autistic children as 'mentally defective' and recommended institutionalization."

Epi's jaw tightened as he read. "That's horrific. These kids were just wired differently. They needed understanding, not exorcism."

"It gets worse," Kayla continued, pulling up more research on her laptop. "The eugenics movement was huge in the 1920s. Oklahoma actually had sterilization laws targeting people they deemed 'mentally defective.' They sterilized over 7,000 people between 1931 and 1963."

The words hit Epi like a physical blow. His hands began to move in the subtle stimming pattern he'd developed—index finger tapping against his thumb in a precise sequence. "They would have sterilized people like me."

"Hans Asperger," Kayla read from another source, "the doctor who first described what we now call Asperger's syndrome, worked directly with the Nazi regime. He sent children he deemed 'uneducable' to Am Spiegelgrund clinic, where they were murdered as part of the 'euthanasia' program. Only the children he thought could be 'useful' to society were spared."

Epi's stimming intensified. The casual mention of children being murdered for being different triggered a flood of memories—not of historical trauma, but of his own, much more recent experiences.

Suddenly he was back in his bedroom six months ago, bathed in the blue glow of his monitor at 11 PM. The Discord server had seemed safe—a community of programmers and tech enthusiasts. But what started as a casual conversation about coding had somehow spiraled into something else when he'd mentioned an innovative algorithm he'd developed.

"Wow, Epi thinks he's the next Turing," one user had typed.
"Bet you think you're superior to everyone else, don't you?"
"Typical autistic savant bullshit."

The comments had escalated quickly, and Epi—exhausted from a long day and not reading the room correctly—had responded with technical explanations that only made things worse. Someone had screenshot his comments, taken them out of context, and within hours they were being circulated as "evidence" of him planning something sinister.

The knock on the door had come at 11:47 PM exactly. Two uniformed officers, their hands resting casually on their weapons, asking to speak with him about "concerning online activity." His parents' faces—the confusion, the fear, the way they'd looked at him like they didn't recognize their own son.

"Epi?" Kayla's voice brought him back to the present. "Are you okay?"

He realized he'd been silent for several minutes, his finger-tapping having accelerated into a rapid pattern that he quickly stopped. "Sorry. Just... processing."

"The eugenics movement wasn't just about 'mental deficiency,'" Kayla continued, unaware of how deeply her research was affecting him. "It was deeply intertwined with racism. They used pseudoscience to justify sterilizing Native Americans, African Americans, anyone they deemed 'unfit.' The same people who wanted to eliminate autism also wanted to eliminate entire racial groups."

"It's funny," Epi said, his voice carefully controlled, "how they called us 'defective' when really, they were afraid of what we could see. Autistic people notice patterns others miss. We call out inconsistencies. We don't just accept 'because that's how it's always been' as an answer."

"That's threatening to people in power," Mark observed.

"Exactly. Now we know that what they called deficits are often superpowers. Pattern recognition, intense focus, innovative thinking, attention to detail—" Epi's voice gained strength. "But it comes without the social filters that make people comfortable. We'll tell you exactly what we think, even when it's inconvenient."

"Is that why you were targeted online?" Kayla asked gently.

Epi's finger-tapping resumed, slower this time. "I corrected someone's code in a public channel. Explained why their approach was inefficient. But I didn't phrase it diplomatically, didn't cushion it with social niceties. To them, I was just being arrogant. They decided to teach me a lesson."

"The police visit," Mark said, understanding.

"They took screenshots of my technical explanations, claimed I was describing how to hack government systems. Completely out of context, but..." Epi shrugged. "Autistic people are easy targets. We say what we mean literally, and then neurotypical people twist our words into something sinister."

"In the 1920s, they would have called you possessed," Kayla said. "In Nazi Germany, they would have killed you. Today, they try to destroy your reputation online."

"Same fear, different methods," Epi agreed. "Fear of minds that work differently."

That evening, they returned to Hope Hall with a new plan. Instead of just investigating, they would try to communicate directly with the trapped spirit.

The boarded window swiveled open as usual, and they made their way to the children's educational wing. The Backpack Magnetometer led them to a room that had obviously been set up as a workshop—tables with built-in vises, tool racks on the walls, and what appeared to be the remnants of mechanical projects.

"Help me, please help me!" The voice was louder here, more desperate.

"We're here to help," Kayla called out gently. "What's your name?"

The ghostly boy materialized more solidly this time, sitting at one of the workbenches with his hands moving in precise, repetitive motions. He was assembling something—gears and springs and tiny mechanical components that appeared and disappeared as his spirit hands worked.

"Timothy," he said without looking up, his gaze fixed on his work with laser-like intensity. "Timothy Ashford. I'm from Enid. I make things. I fix things. But I can't fix this."

Epi recognized the hyperfocus immediately—the way Timothy's entire world had narrowed to the mechanical components in front of him. It was exactly how he felt when coding, when the outside world ceased to exist and there was only the elegant logic of the algorithm.

"What can't you fix, Timothy?" Epi asked, recognizing a kindred spirit.

"The fear. The pain. They said I was possessed by the devil because I couldn't look at faces. Because I had to count things. Because sounds hurt my ears." Timothy's hands never stopped moving as he spoke, the repetitive motion clearly soothing to him. "My parents brought a preacher. He said the devil made me different. That I needed to be cleansed."

"Timothy," Epi said gently, "there's nothing wrong with your brain. You're not possessed. You're autistic. It's a neurological difference, not a curse."

Timothy's hands stilled for a moment, and he glanced up briefly. "Autistic?"

"It means your brain processes information differently than most people's. You notice details others miss. You can focus intensely on things that interest you. You understand systems and patterns in ways that seem almost magical to neurotypical people."

Mark stepped closer, his voice gentle. "Timothy, what happened to bring you here?"

"Dr. Morrison saved me. He found me after the exorcism went wrong. After they..." Timothy's hands resumed their frantic motion. "After they tried to beat the demons out of me. Held me down while the preacher shouted and pressed crosses into my skin until they burned. Dr. Morrison brought me here and said I could work with my hands. He said I wasn't possessed—I was gifted."

64

Epi felt his chest tighten. The casual description of religious trauma inflicted on a child for being different hit too close to home. He remembered his own childhood, the endless attempts to "fix" him, to make him more "normal."

"What did you make?" Kayla asked, looking at the ghostly tools and components.

Timothy smiled—the first peaceful expression they'd seen from him. "Clocks. Music boxes. Mechanical toys for the other children. Dr. Morrison said my brain worked like the most beautiful machine ever created. He said I could see the music in mathematics, the poetry in precision."

"Then what went wrong?" Epi asked softly, though he was dreading the answer.

Timothy's expression darkened. "The accident. I was working on a special project—a clockwork turtle that could walk and move its head. I was so focused, so deep in the work, that I didn't hear the whistle. Didn't hear them calling for the end of workshop time."

Epi understood immediately. The hyperfocus that was both gift and curse—the ability to become so absorbed in a task that the rest of the world disappeared entirely.

"The power saw. I was adjusting the mechanism, and my sleeve caught in the blade. Dr. Morrison found me. He held my hand while..." Timothy looked down at his ghostly form, where his right arm ended abruptly at the wrist.

"You died from the injury," Mark said quietly.

"But I never finished the turtle," Timothy said, his voice breaking. "It was for Billy Morrison—Dr. Morrison's nephew. The boy who died in the fire. I wanted to make something beautiful for him, something that would make him happy. But I failed. I always fail."

"You didn't fail," Epi said firmly. "Timothy, what if I told you that your work didn't fail? What if I told you that brilliant minds like yours went on to create amazing things?"

"What do you mean?"

Epi pulled out his tablet, showing Timothy images of modern robotics, computers, and mechanical engineering marvels. "People who think like you—who see patterns and mechanisms that others miss—they built the modern world. Temple Grandin revolutionized animal welfare design. Dan Aykroyd created one of the most successful comedy franchises in history. Satoshi Tajiri created Pokémon because of his intense interest in collecting insects."

Timothy stared at the images with wonder. "These machines... they're so complex. So beautiful."

"And many were created by people with autism," Kayla added. "Timothy, your difference wasn't a curse. It was a gift. The same intense focus that got you in trouble also gave you the ability to create mechanical marvels that no neurotypical thirteen-year-old could have conceived."

Epi leaned forward, his voice passionate. "Do you know what they call us now? The autism spectrum. Because we're not broken—we're just operating on a different frequency. Some of us are brilliant engineers, others are mathematical savants, still others can see patterns in data that nobody else notices."

"But they tried to exorcise me," Timothy whispered.

"Because they were afraid," Epi said. "Afraid of minds that work differently. Afraid of people who see things they can't see, who notice details they miss, who won't just smile and nod when something doesn't make sense."

The Backpack Magnetometer's tone shifted from frantic clicking to something more musical, more harmonious—the sound of multiple frequencies finding resonance.

"I understand now," Timothy said, his ghostly form becoming more solid and peaceful. "I wasn't broken. I was just... different. And different can be wonderful."

"Your turtle," Epi said suddenly. "Show me how it was supposed to work."

Timothy's eyes lit up as he began describing the intricate clockwork mechanisms he'd designed. As he spoke, the phantom components on his workbench began to move, assembling themselves into the shape of a mechanical turtle.

"The head turns on a cam mechanism," Timothy explained excitedly, his hands moving with renewed purpose. "And the legs move in a walking pattern controlled by this gear train. See? It's all about the timing of the movements. The mathematics of motion translated into mechanical poetry."

The ghostly turtle began to walk across the workbench, its head turning from side to side with lifelike curiosity. It was a masterpiece of mechanical engineering, especially considering it had been designed by a thirteen-year-old boy with 1920s technology.

"It's beautiful, Timothy," Kayla breathed. "It's absolutely beautiful."

"Billy would have loved it," Timothy said, his voice filled with satisfaction rather than regret.

As he spoke, another ghostly figure appeared—Billy Morrison, the boy who had died in the fire. He reached out to touch the mechanical turtle, his face filled with wonder and joy.

"Timothy! You did finish it! You made the most wonderful toy I've ever seen!"

The two ghost boys embraced, and suddenly the workshop was filled with the spirits of other children—kids who had benefited from Timothy's mechanical toys and inventions during his time at Hope Hall.

"You brought us so much happiness," Billy said. "Your creations were the bright spots in our dark time here. The music box that played lullabies for the scared children. The clockwork bird that made the sick kids laugh. The puzzle boxes that kept our minds busy when the sadness was too much."

Timothy looked around at all the children, then back at Kayla, Epi, and Mark. "I remember now. I wasn't a failure. I was a creator. I brought joy to others through my work."

"And you proved that autistic minds aren't defective," Epi added. "You proved that we're innovative, creative, capable of beauty that neurotypical minds might never conceive."

The ghostly workshop began to fade, but not with sadness. Instead, it dissolved into points of light that swirled around the room like stars, finally coalescing into a warm, golden glow before disappearing entirely.

The next day, they found Timothy—the real Timothy—sitting on a park bench near Cimarron Drive, watching turtles on the creek bank. He was about twelve years old, wearing modern clothes, and very much alive.

"Hey," Kayla said gently, sitting beside him. "Watching the turtles?"

"They're amazing," Timothy said without looking at her, his voice carrying the same precise intonation they'd heard from his ghost. "Did you know their shells are actually modified ribcages? The engineering is incredible. The way the scutes overlap for maximum protection while maintaining flexibility..."

A group of older kids nearby were calling out taunts: "Turtle boy! Hey, turtle freak! What's wrong with you?"

"They don't understand," Timothy said matter-of-factly, his fingers moving in a subtle stimming pattern. "But that's okay. I'm designing a turtle-themed video game. The mechanics are really complex."

Epi sat down on Timothy's other side. "What kind of game mechanics?"

Timothy's face lit up as he began describing his ideas— intricate systems involving shell physics, aquatic navigation, and ecosystem management. His hands moved as he talked, sketching invisible diagrams in the air. As he spoke, Kayla noticed him discretely adding what looked like malicious code to a notebook.

"Timothy," she said carefully, "what's that you're writing?"

"Oh, this? Just some extra features for kids who are mean to other kids. Nothing permanent. Just... inconvenient."
Timothy's smile was perfectly innocent, but there was a glint in his eyes that suggested his revenge would be both creative and precisely calibrated.

Mark chuckled. "Remind me never to get on your bad side."

"You're different like us," Epi said. "That's not a bad thing. That's what makes you brilliant. In the past, they would have called you possessed. In some places, they would have tried to cure you or worse. But now we know better. We know that autistic minds are some of the most innovative, creative minds on the planet."

Timothy finally looked at them directly, a small smile playing at the corners of his mouth. "You really think so?"

"We know so," Kayla said firmly. "The world needs minds like yours. People who see systems differently, who notice what others miss, who can focus with laser intensity on solving problems."

"Just remember," Epi added, thinking of his own online experiences, "be careful who you trust with your ideas. Not everyone appreciates different minds, even today."

Timothy nodded seriously. "I know. That's why I'm building in... security features."

As they walked away, leaving Timothy to his turtle observations and game design—and whatever elaborate digital revenge he was plotting—Kayla felt a profound sense of completion. They had helped two versions of the same soul: one trapped in the past by trauma and misunderstanding, and one living in the present with the potential for a brilliant future.

Behind them, a real turtle poked its head out of the creek, looked directly at Timothy, and seemed to nod before disappearing back into the water.

"You know," Epi said as they reached the parking lot, "What happened to me was almost like the "SWATTING that people do to get the police to raid and arrest someone they're upset with. It's so dangerous. I almost stepped away from programming and designing things. I almost left."

"But you're still here," Kayla pointed out.

"Yeah," Epi smiled, thinking of Timothy—both versions of him. "We're still here. And we're still creating things they can't even imagine."

EPISODE 6: ANOREXIA AND THE FLAPPER AND THE FLYER

"She's so tiny," Kayla said, watching the cheerleader practice squad from the university gym's bleachers. The girl in question—a "flyer" who was launched into the air during routines—couldn't have weighed more than eighty-five pounds soaking wet. Her name was Jessica, and when she spoke to her teammates, her voice was impossibly sweet and high-pitched, like a cartoon character come to life.

"Did you see my latest TikTok?" Jessica chirped to the girl beside her, her delicate hands fluttering as she pulled out her phone. "Forty thousand likes! The comments are so sweet— everyone's saying how 'goals' my body is and how they wish they could be as disciplined as me."

But even as she smiled and giggled with her teammates, something darker flickered behind Jessica's eyes. The sweet voice that spoke aloud was constantly being drowned out by another voice—a deep, commanding presence that lived inside her head.

You're still too heavy, the dark voice growled. *Look at your thighs touching when you sit. Disgusting. The bases are struggling to hold you. You need to lose five more pounds. Ten more pounds. You need to disappear.*

Mark nodded grimly, watching Jessica stand and immediately check her reflection in the mirrored wall. "She fainted yesterday during practice and just barely avoided serious injury. The scary part is, she's actually gotten weaker—last year she was stable in the air, but now she's so frail that she can't control her body during stunts. They want the flyers to be as light as possible, but they don't realize that below a certain weight, the flyers become liabilities."

"That's insane," Kayla muttered, studying the girl's stick-thin arms and hollow cheeks. The definition of "dangerously thin" for someone Jessica's height—about 5'2"—was generally considered anything below 95 pounds, putting her vital organs at risk. But for a competitive athlete performing high-impact stunts, the threshold was even higher. "She's starving herself for a sport that requires strength."

Jessica's phone buzzed with notifications. Her latest Instagram post—a photo of her in her cheer uniform with the caption "Flying high! ✦ #flyer #goals #discipline"—was blowing up. But mixed in with the praise were the cruel comments that fed the dark voice in her head:

"Looking chunky in this pic ngl" "Maybe lay off the carbs if you want to actually FLY lmao" "Too fat to be a flyer tbh"

The sweet-voiced Jessica would normally brush off such comments, but the monster inside her seized on them like fuel. *See?* the dark voice hissed. *Even strangers can see how disgusting you are. You need to cut calories again. Skip dinner. Skip breakfast. You don't deserve food.*

What Jessica didn't know was that last year's "minor head injury" during a failed stunt hadn't been the concussion everyone thought. The impact had caused a small but significant brain bleed that went undetected. Her weakened state—bones brittle from malnutrition, muscles atrophied

74

from under-eating—had made what should have been a routine dismount into a life-threatening fall.

That evening over dinner, Kayla brought up the subject with her mother. "Mom, when did this obsession with thinness start? I mean, when did being skinny become more important than being healthy?"

Dr. Garvin paused with her fork halfway to her mouth. "Well, there was Twiggy in the 1960s. But really, it goes back much further. It's all about perfectionism—or control. Though social media has weaponized it in ways we've never seen before."

"But I don't think it's just about perfectionism," Kayla disagreed. "What if it's about not wanting to change into what your destiny—your biology—is pushing you toward? Like starving to forestall puberty?"

"That's... actually a very insightful observation," her mother said slowly. "The irony is that extreme caloric restriction actually delays puberty and can cause amenorrhea—the cessation of menstruation. It's the body's way of saying it doesn't have enough resources to support reproduction."

"Has this always been the case, do you think?"

"I don't know, but I'm going to find out." Kayla pulled out her phone and began researching. "Mom, did you know that suffragettes in England went on hunger strikes starting in

1909? When they were arrested for protesting, they refused to eat in jail."

"And they were force-fed," Dr. Garvin said, her expression darkening. "I remember reading about that. They pushed tubes down their throats and forced milk and egg mixtures into their stomachs. It was medieval torture disguised as medical treatment."

"Emmeline Pankhurst was jailed for two months in 1912 for throwing a rock at 10 Downing Street. She went on hunger strike too." Kayla's research was revealing disturbing parallels. "The suffragettes considered hunger strikes to be valiant. They gave out medals to survivors at special meetings. But here's the thing—the newspapers ate it up. The more dramatic the hunger strikes became, the more coverage they got."

Dr. Garvin set down her fork. "Media attention as reinforcement. The same pattern we see with social media today."

"Exactly. And I found something else disturbing—some historians think that after the suffragette movement ended, some of the women who had used hunger strikes as political weapons found they couldn't stop the behavior. They'd essentially trained themselves to use food restriction as a form of control, and it became compulsive."

"A proto-eating disorder," Dr. Garvin mused. "The line between political resistance and psychological compulsion."

"And women could be committed to places like Hope Hall for 'defiance disorder' or for their behavior as activists," Dr. Garvin added. "Kayla, are you thinking what I think you're thinking?"

"We need to go back to Hope Hall. If they force-fed suffragettes and other women there, there might be spirits who can help us understand what's really happening with girls like Jessica."

Two nights later, Kayla, Epi, and Minzie made their way through the familiar corridors of Hope Hall. The Backpack Magnetometer led them to a wing they hadn't explored before—one that the hospital blueprints labeled simply as "Women's Disciplinary."

"This feels different from the other places," Minzie observed. "Angrier."

The air was thick with the residual energy of rage and desperation. Unlike the sad acceptance they'd felt in the children's wing or the peaceful resolution in the therapy areas, this place pulsed with defiance and barely contained fury.

"Look at this," Epi said, shining his flashlight on marks scratched into the wall. "These are dates. And names. 'Alice Morrison - 1913 - Votes for Women.' 'Sarah Campbell - 1915 - Refused to obey husband.' 'Margaret Stevens - 1917 - Immoral conduct.'"

"They were imprisoned here for fighting for their rights," Kayla said, running her fingers over the scratched messages. Each name represented a woman whose crime was wanting more from life than society was willing to give her.

A low moaning echoed through the corridor, followed by the sound of retching and violent struggling. They followed the sounds to a room lined with metal chairs, each equipped with leather restraints and ominous-looking metal devices.

"Force-feeding room," Minzie whispered, horrified.

A ghostly woman materialized in one of the chairs, her arms and legs strapped down, her head held in place by a cruel metal brace that forced her mouth open. A spectral nurse stood beside her, holding a thick rubber tube with the mechanical efficiency of someone who had performed this torture countless times.

"No!" the woman screamed, her voice raw from previous sessions. "I will not eat! I will not submit! Votes for women! You cannot break my will!"

The ghostly nurse forced the tube down the woman's throat, and the spirit convulsed in agony as phantom liquid was poured into her stomach. Her body jerked against the restraints, her eyes wild with panic and rage.

"Stop!" Kayla shouted. "You don't have to relive this!"

The woman's eyes focused on them, and the horrible scene paused. "You... you can see us?"

"Yes. We're here to help. What's your name?"

"Margaret Worthington. I was arrested in London for chaining myself to the Prime Minister's residence. They deported me back to America, but my husband had me committed here for 'hysteria and defiance.'" Her voice carried the refined accent of education and privilege, which made her imprisonment here all the more tragic.

"Why won't you eat?" Epi asked gently.

Margaret's ghostly form sat up straighter, despite the restraints. "Because eating means surrendering. It means accepting their authority over my body, my choices, my voice. As long as I refuse food, I retain the one power they cannot take from me—the power to say no. In prison, we discovered that hunger strikes were our most powerful weapon. The press couldn't ignore them."

"But the press attention," Kayla said carefully, "did it ever feel like... like you had to keep escalating to maintain their interest?"

Margaret's expression flickered. "The newspapers did love a dramatic story. The longer we held out, the more heroic they made us sound. There was pressure to... to prove our dedication through suffering. Some of us began competing to see who could last longest."

"But you're hurting yourself," Minzie said.

"Better to die free than live enslaved," Margaret replied fiercely, but something in her voice suggested she'd repeated this phrase so many times it had become automatic. "Every day I refuse to eat is another day I prove they cannot break my will."

Another spirit materialized—a younger woman in 1920s flapper clothing, her dress hanging loose on her skeletal frame. When she spoke, her voice carried the same hollow quality as Jessica's sweet chirping.

"But Margaret, what happens when the refusal becomes the prison? When you can't remember how to say yes to anything? When the voice in your head becomes louder than your own voice?"

"Who are you?" Kayla asked.

"Dorothy Fleming. I came here in 1923. I was a flapper—I danced, I drank, I kissed boys, I voted. My father said I was 'morally corrupt' and had me committed." Dorothy gestured to her gaunt frame, her movements bird-like and fragile. "I stopped eating to punish them. To show them they couldn't control me. But after a while... I couldn't stop. Even when I wanted to."

"You developed anorexia," Kayla said softly.

"Is that what you call it now? I called it 'fading away.' It started as rebellion, but it became... something else. A way to disappear rather than fight. The voice inside my head—it was so much louder than my own voice. It told me I was

80

disgusting, that I took up too much space, that I didn't deserve food or love or even existence."

Dorothy looked directly at Kayla with haunted eyes. "You know a girl like this now, don't you? A girl who seems sweet on the outside but has a monster living inside her head?"

Kayla thought of Jessica's chirpy voice and bright smile, and the darkness she'd glimpsed flickering behind her eyes. "Yes. She's a cheerleader. A flyer. She's gotten so thin that she's actually becoming dangerous in the air—too weak to control her own body during stunts."

"The modern newspapers—they're in everyone's pockets now, aren't they?" Margaret asked, materializing more fully. "These 'social media' platforms?"

"Yes," Minzie said. "And they're crueler than anything you faced. Anonymous strangers can say horrible things about a girl's appearance twenty-four hours a day."

"And the praise is just as dangerous," Epi added. "When Jessica posts photos of herself looking extremely thin, she gets thousands of likes and comments telling her she's 'goals' and 'perfect.' It reinforces the behavior just like newspaper coverage reinforced hunger strikes."

Margaret and Dorothy looked at each other across the decades, two women whose resistance had taken different forms but led to similar suffering.

"The young women now," Margaret said, her ghostly gaze fixed on Kayla. "The ones who starve themselves—are they fighting something too?"

"I think so," Kayla replied. "They're fighting pressure to be perfect, pressure to be small, pressure to take up less space in the world. But they're also fighting their own biology—their bodies' natural development into adult women."

"But they're making themselves smaller instead of making the world bigger," Dorothy observed sadly. "We fought to expand women's possibilities. They're contracting their own existence. I became so obsessed with control that I lost control entirely."

"The cheerleader," Minzie said suddenly. "Jessica. She's not just trying to be light enough to fly. She's trying to disappear entirely. And the more positive feedback she gets for being tiny, the more the monster inside her head demands."

The Backpack Magnetometer began emitting a different tone—not the frantic clicking of trauma, but a steady, purposeful rhythm that seemed to resonate with both past and present suffering.

"What happens when someone gets too thin to safely perform athletics?" Epi asked the spirits.

Dorothy's form flickered. "In my time, girls simply died. Quietly, in their beds, their hearts giving out. Or they had 'accidents'—fainting and falling down stairs, bones breaking from the slightest impact."

"Jessica almost died last year," Kayla said. "What everyone thought was a minor head injury was actually a brain bleed. Her body was too weak to withstand what should have been a routine stunt."

"And yet she continues," Margaret said grimly. "Because the voice inside her head is louder than the voice of reason. Because she's addicted to the control, even as it destroys her."

"What can we do?" Kayla asked the spirits. "How do we help girls who are trapped in the same cycle?"

Margaret stood up, her restraints dissolving. "You tell them that their bodies belong to them. Not to coaches, not to parents, not to society, not to anonymous strangers on the internet. Theirs. And you remind them that making themselves smaller won't make their problems smaller—it just makes them too weak to fight."

Dorothy joined her, her flapper dress becoming more solid and vibrant. "And you tell them that rebellion should expand their world, not contract it. If they want to fight the system, they need to be strong enough to fight. The monster voice inside their heads—it's not their voice. It's the voice of everyone who wants them to disappear."

"The suffragettes who survived," Margaret added, "we learned to eat strategically. Not in surrender, but as fuel for the battle. Food became our ammunition. We realized that a starving woman can't change the world—she can barely change her own circumstances."

"Tell them," Dorothy said, her voice growing stronger, "that the goal isn't to disappear. The goal is to become so magnificently, undeniably present that the world has no choice but to make room for them."

As the spirits began to fade, Margaret offered one final warning: "And tell them to be wary of the praise. The voices that call them 'perfect' when they're wasting away—those voices want them weak. True allies will celebrate their strength, not their disappearance."

The next day, Kayla volunteered to help with the cheerleading squad's nutrition education program. When she saw Jessica—barely visible in her oversized team sweatshirt—she sat down beside her during break.

"You know," Kayla said casually, "I've been learning about the suffragettes. Did you know they went on hunger strikes, but then figured out that they needed to eat strategically?"

Jessica looked up from her untouched protein bar, her sweet voice at odds with the exhaustion in her eyes. "What do you mean?"

"I mean the media loved covering their hunger strikes—it made for dramatic headlines. But the suffragettes realized that the attention was becoming more important than the cause. And they figured out that starving themselves gave their opponents exactly what they wanted—weak women who couldn't fight back."

Jessica's phone buzzed with another cruel comment: *"Still looking chunky. When are you going to take this seriously?"*

But for the first time, instead of the monster voice seizing on the cruelty, Jessica heard something else—the memory of her own voice from before the monster had moved in.

"The real rebellion," Kayla continued, "isn't making yourself smaller. It's making yourself strong enough to change the rules. Strong enough to tell that voice in your head—the one that sounds like all your worst critics rolled into one—to shut up."

Jessica stared at the protein bar in her hands. "What if... what if I can't tell the difference anymore between my voice and the other voice?"

"Then you start small," Kayla said gently. "You take one bite. And you tell yourself that this bite is fuel for battle, not surrender. That feeding yourself is an act of rebellion against everyone who wants you to disappear."

That afternoon, Jessica ate the protein bar. Then she ate lunch. And when the coach made his usual comment about her needing to "watch her weight," she looked him straight in the eye and said, "I'm not watching my weight. I'm building my strength. And if you want me to fly safely, you're going to have to deal with me at fighting weight."

The monster voice roared in protest, but for the first time in months, Jessica's own voice was louder.

In the distance, barely visible against the afternoon sky, two ghostly figures—a suffragette in practical dress and a flapper in beaded silk—raised their hands in victory salutes before fading into the Oklahoma sunshine.

Author's Note: Anorexia nervosa has the highest mortality rate of any mental health disorder. If you or someone you know is struggling with an eating disorder, please reach out to the National Eating Disorders Association (NEDA) at 1-800-931-2237 or visit nationaleatingdisorders.org.

EPISODE 7: GLOVE MAN

Kayla woke with a start, her heart pounding like a trapped bird against her ribs. In her dream—or was it a dream?—pale hands in white gloves had slipped through the spindles of her wooden headboard, fingers slowly closing around her throat. The sensation had been so real she could still feel the phantom pressure against her windpipe, the cotton fabric rough against her skin.

She sat up in bed, checking her phone: 3:17 AM. Outside her window, the university campus was quiet except for the distant sound of someone walking. The footsteps were regular, methodical, as if someone were pacing the same route over and over. Through the glass, she could see the ancient oak trees of Norman swaying in the humid Oklahoma night, their leaves rustling with secrets. The sky was overcast, heavy with the promise of another summer storm, the kind that turned the red dirt to mud and made the air taste of copper and ozone.

The dream had stirred something in her chest—a familiar tightness she'd been pushing down for months. The feeling of hands around her throat wasn't entirely foreign. Sometimes, late at night, she felt her own invisible hands there, squeezing, punishing.

Stop it, she told herself, the same words she'd repeated every night for... how long had it been now? *It wasn't your fault. You couldn't have known.*

But the rational part of her mind was always weakest at 3 AM, when the thing she refused to think about pressed against her consciousness like water against a cracking dam.

The next morning at breakfast, she described the dream to her mother, carefully omitting the part about how real it had felt, how it had made her remember things she'd rather forget.

"White gloves?" Dr. Garvin paused with her coffee cup halfway to her lips. "That's... oddly specific. You know, when I was researching the Hope Hall records, I came across mentions of a patient they called 'Glove Man.' He walked miles around Norman every day, always wearing white gloves, often talking to himself."

"What was wrong with him?"

"According to the files, he was convinced his hands were deformed. But the medical examinations showed his hands were perfectly normal. It was a delusion, but a powerful one. He refused to remove the gloves under any circumstances." Dr. Garvin set down her cup, her expression thoughtful. "The file mentioned something about survivor's guilt—apparently he'd witnessed some kind of industrial accident. Back then, they didn't understand the connection between trauma and somatic delusions."

Kayla's hand involuntarily moved to her throat, then quickly dropped to her lap. "That's so sad. What happened to him?"

"The records are incomplete, but apparently he was released as an outpatient. He continued his daily walks around town, always wearing the gloves. People just got used to seeing him. There's actually a fascinating historical parallel—Lady Macbeth's obsessive hand-washing, you know? Shakespeare understood something about guilt and compulsive behavior that psychiatry wouldn't formally recognize for another 300 years."

"Mom, if he were alive today, no one would even notice him talking to himself. Everyone would assume he was on a phone call."

Dr. Garvin smiled, but her eyes remained concerned. She'd noticed her daughter's nervous habits lately—the way Kayla's hands would flutter to her throat when she thought no one was looking, the way she'd grown quieter, more withdrawn. "You're probably right. Amazing how context changes everything. Though sometimes I wonder if we're just better at hiding our madness now, not actually healing it."

Outside, the morning sky hung low and gray, pressing down on the campus like a weighted blanket. The old elm trees that lined the quad drooped in the still air, their leaves already showing the stress of another brutal Oklahoma summer. Even the mockingbirds seemed subdued, their usual chatter reduced to occasional, halfhearted trills.

That evening, Kayla shared the story with Epi and Mark as they prepared for another investigation at Hope Hall. The three of them had developed an easy rhythm over the past weeks, though Kayla noticed that Epi's equipment seemed to be getting more sensitive—or perhaps more attuned to something specific.

"Delusions about body parts being deformed," Epi mused, adjusting his Backpack Magnetometer. The device had been behaving strangely lately, its electromagnetic readings spiking in patterns that seemed almost... organic. "That's actually a recognized condition now—body dysmorphic disorder. But it's interesting how it manifests differently based on the underlying trauma. Some people see flaws that aren't there, others see stains, marks, signs of guilt."

"The question is," Mark said, "what traumatized him enough to create such a specific delusion? And why is he showing up in Kayla's dreams?"

Kayla's hand moved to her throat again, a gesture so automatic she didn't realize she was doing it. "Maybe some ghosts are just drawn to... to people who understand what they're going through."

Epi glanced at her sharply. His device was producing unusual readings—not just electromagnetic fluctuations, but something deeper, more complex. The patterns reminded him of interference waves, as if multiple emotional frequencies were being compressed, distorted. He'd been tracking these anomalies for weeks, and they always seemed strongest when Kayla was present, but there was something else—a strange dampening effect, as if powerful emotions were being actively suppressed.

"Historically speaking," Epi continued, trying to keep his voice casual while monitoring his equipment, "guilt-induced madness has been documented for centuries. Look at Caravaggio—after he killed a man in a tennis match, he fled Rome and spent the rest of his short life painting increasingly dark, violent scenes. Some scholars think his guilt literally drove him mad. Or Emperor Caligula, who supposedly went insane after being forced to watch his family members die. The Romans understood that guilt could be as destructive as any physical poison."

"You're saying guilt can actually break a person's mind?" Mark asked.

"Not just break it—reshape it entirely. The brain will create elaborate justifications, visual hallucinations, compulsive behaviors, anything to try to process unbearable shame." Epi's magnetometer was now emitting a low, steady whine. "Sometimes I think strong emotions create their own electromagnetic signatures. But when they're repressed, compressed, the energy gets... distorted. Like trying to hold back a flood with a dam that's already cracking."

Kayla felt a chill that had nothing to do with the evening air. "That's a disturbing thought."

"What's disturbing is how the distortion seems to call to similar frequencies," Epi said, but his attention was focused on his device. The readings were unlike anything he'd ever seen—layers of electromagnetic activity, some clear and strong, others buried deep and compressed, as if someone were trying to broadcast and jam a signal at the same time.

The boarded window swiveled open as usual, and they made their way through the familiar corridors. Tonight, the building felt different—heavier, more oppressive. Outside, the wind had picked up, sending the branches of the old cottonwoods scraping against the windows like skeletal fingers. The approaching storm had turned the sky a deep purple-black, and occasional flashes of lightning illuminated the peeling paint on the walls.

The Backpack Magnetometer led them to a wing they hadn't explored—one that housed patients with physical disabilities and those who were considered "incurable." The hallway was longer than the others, with more windows. During the day, it would have been filled with natural light—a design choice meant to combat depression in long-term patients.

"Listen," Kayla whispered.

Footsteps echoed through the corridor—steady, repetitive, the sound of someone walking the same path endlessly. The steps were accompanied by a low murmuring, like someone carrying on a conversation with an invisible companion.

"He's still walking," Mark observed. "After all these years, he's still walking."

Kayla pressed her back against the wall, her breathing shallow. The sound of the footsteps was triggering something deep inside her—a memory she kept locked away, buried under layers of rationalization and forced normalcy. Her chest tightened with the familiar weight of something unnamed, something she couldn't—wouldn't—let herself examine too closely.

Epi noticed her distress and glanced at his equipment. The readings were spiking again, but in that strange, compressed way he'd been observing. It was as if massive amounts of emotional energy were being generated but then immediately suppressed, creating interference patterns in the electromagnetic field. Whatever Kayla was carrying inside, she was fighting very hard to keep it buried.

They followed the sounds to what had once been a day room—a large, open space with tall windows and built-in benches. Through the windows, they could see the storm approaching, the cottonwood trees bending almost horizontal in the wind. A ghostly figure paced back and forth across the room, his path worn into the spectral floorboards by decades of repetition.

The man was in his thirties, wearing the simple gray uniform of a Hope Hall patient. But most striking were his hands—encased in pristine white gloves that seemed to glow with their own light.

"Sir?" Kayla called gently, her voice barely audible over the rising wind. "Could we speak with you?"

The pacing stopped. The man turned toward them, and they could see his face clearly for the first time. It was a kind face, intelligent but haunted, with eyes that held deep shame and confusion. Something about his expression made Kayla's breath catch not recognition exactly, but a resonance, as if she were looking at something she understood on a level she couldn't quite name.

"You can see me?" he asked, his voice carrying a slight tremor.

"Yes. We're here to help. What's your name?"

"Theodore Whitman. But everyone calls me Glove Man." He held up his hands, studying them through the white fabric. "I can't let anyone see. They're too horrible to look at."

Kayla found herself unconsciously wrapping her arms around herself, a protective gesture that had become automatic whenever she felt the edges of her carefully maintained composure beginning to fray.

"Theodore," Epi said carefully, his device now humming at a frequency that seemed to harmonize with Theodore's anguish, "can you tell us what's wrong with your hands?"

Theodore's expression crumpled. "They're... they're stained. Marked. Cursed. If people saw them, they'd know what I did. They'd know I'm a coward who let people die."

Something twisted in Kayla's chest—a sharp, familiar pain that she immediately pushed down. *Not now,* she told herself. *Don't think about it now.*

"What did you do?" she asked gently, though part of her was afraid to hear the answer.

Theodore resumed pacing, his agitation increasing. Outside, the storm finally broke, sending sheets of rain against the windows. "The factory. I worked at the cotton mill in

94

Oklahoma City. There was an accident—the machinery caught fire. It was 1924, and safety regulations were... different then. People were trapped."

He stopped pacing and stared at his gloved hands. "I could have saved them. There was a lever—an emergency shut-off. But I was scared. The fire was so close, and I could hear the screaming, and I just... I ran. Like a coward. Like someone who values his own life over others."

Kayla's composure finally cracked. The words hit her like physical blows, each one striking against the walls she'd built around her own buried trauma.

"How many people died?" Mark asked quietly.

"Seventeen. Seventeen people died because I was a coward. Because I saved myself instead of pulling that lever." Theodore's voice broke. "Their blood is on my hands. Literally. I can see it. Dark stains that never wash off. Sometimes I dream about them—their faces in the flames, calling my name, asking why I didn't save them."

Epi's magnetometer was producing increasingly complex readings, multiple frequencies layering and interfering with each other. He glanced at Kayla and saw her struggling to maintain control, her face pale and her hands trembling. The equipment was detecting something extraordinary—two powerful emotional resonances, one ancient and fully expressed, the other fresh and desperately contained.

"Theodore," Kayla said softly, her voice thick with emotion, "you were scared. That's not a crime. That's human."

"But I lived when they didn't!" he cried. "I had the power to save them, and I chose not to use it! Every day since then, I've walked and walked, trying to... to wear away the guilt. Trying to punish myself enough that maybe the dead will forgive me."

Kayla stepped forward, her voice tight with barely controlled emotion. "What happened after the fire?"

"I couldn't function. Couldn't work, couldn't eat, couldn't sleep. I kept staring at my hands, seeing the blood, feeling the heat. My family thought I was going insane. Maybe I was." Theodore held up his gloved hands. "These hide the stains. As long as I wear them, people can't see what I really am."

"But there are no stains," Mark said. "Theodore, there never were any stains. The guilt you feel—that's in your mind, not on your hands."

Theodore shook his head violently. "You can't know that. You haven't seen them without the gloves. You haven't lived with this for a hundred years."

"Then show us," Kayla challenged, her voice strained. "If the stains are real, show us."

She stopped abruptly, biting back words that wanted to spill out, secrets that pressed against her consciousness like water against a dam. The effort of containing them made her physically shake.

Epi's equipment was producing increasingly complex readings, layers of electromagnetic interference that suggested multiple emotional frequencies trying to occupy the same space. Whatever was happening, it was bigger than just Theodore's manifestation—it was as if the ghost was being drawn to something equally powerful but hidden, compressed, fighting to stay buried.

For a long moment, Theodore stood frozen. Then, slowly, he began to peel off one glove. As the white fabric fell away, they could see his ghostly hand clearly—pale, long-fingered, completely unmarked.

"There's nothing there," Epi said gently, though his mind was racing. His device was detecting something unprecedented— two distinct emotional signatures, one fully manifested as Theodore's spirit, the other compressed and hidden but equally powerful. Whatever Kayla was carrying, it was calling to Theodore's guilt like a magnet, but she was fighting desperately to keep it contained. "Your hands are clean, Theodore."

Theodore stared at his exposed hand in amazement. "But... but I can see..."

"You see what guilt tells you to see," Kayla explained, her voice carefully controlled despite the tears threatening to spill over. "Theodore, you survived something terrible. That doesn't make you evil. It makes you human. It makes you..." She took a careful breath, not trusting herself to say more. "It makes you someone who has to find a way to live with impossible weight."

"But the seventeen people—"

"Would probably want you to live," Mark interrupted. "Would want you to be happy. Would want you to forgive yourself and use the rest of your life to honor their memory."

Theodore slowly removed the second glove. Both hands were clean, unmarked, free of the phantom stains that had tormented him for decades.

"I've been walking these halls for so long," he whispered. "Walking and walking, trying to wear away the guilt. But it never worked."

"Because guilt isn't something you can walk away from," Kayla said, her voice stronger now but still carefully measured. "It's something you have to face and then... and then find a way to carry without letting it consume you completely."

The storm outside was reaching its peak, the wind howling through the broken windows of Hope Hall. But inside the day room, something was shifting. The Backpack Magnetometer's tone was changing from agitated clicking to something more peaceful, more resolved.

"The contemporary counterpart," Epi said suddenly, pieces clicking into place in his mind. "Theodore, do you know there are people today who suffer from the same kind of delusions? People who think their bodies are wrong or marked in ways that others can't see?"

"Really?"

"Really. And there are treatments now. Ways to help people see their bodies as they really are, not as trauma tells them they are. Cognitive behavioral therapy, exposure therapy, medications that can help quiet the voices of guilt and shame."

Theodore looked around the day room where he'd been pacing for decades. "All this time, I've been punishing myself for being human. For being afraid. For surviving when others didn't."

"It's time to stop," Kayla said firmly, though she wasn't entirely sure she was speaking only to Theodore. "It's time to forgive yourself and find peace."

Theodore nodded slowly, then began to fade—not with the violence of being banished, but with the peaceful dissolution of a burden finally released. As he disappeared, his voice echoed one final time: "Tell them... tell people like me... that being human isn't a crime. That survival isn't a sin. That sometimes the bravest thing you can do is keep living."

The next day dawned clear and bright, the storm having washed the air clean. The campus looked renewed, the old elm trees standing tall and proud, their leaves glistening with raindrops. Even the mockingbirds seemed more cheerful, their songs ringing clear across the quad.

They encountered a young man on campus sitting alone, obsessively washing his hands at an outdoor fountain. His hands were red and raw from constant scrubbing, but he couldn't seem to stop. The scene was achingly familiar—Kayla had spent countless hours at her own sink, scrubbing until her skin was raw, trying to wash away something that existed only in her mind.

"Hey," Kayla said, approaching carefully. "Are you okay?"

The young man looked up with eyes that held the same shame and confusion they'd seen in Theodore's ghost. "I can't get them clean," he whispered. "No matter how much I wash them, I can't get them clean."

"What are you trying to wash off?" Epi asked gently, his magnetometer silent for once.

"The accident. I was driving when... when it happened. It wasn't my fault, the police said so, but I can still feel it. The impact. The blood. It won't come off."

Kayla sat down beside him, her heart racing with recognition. "What if I told you," she said carefully, "that feeling guilty for surviving doesn't honor the people who were hurt? What if I told you that sometimes the hardest thing isn't... isn't what happened, but learning how to keep living afterward?"

The young man stopped scrubbing and looked at his raw, damaged hands. "But how do I stop seeing it? How do I stop feeling responsible?"

Kayla was quiet for a long moment, staring at the fountain's clear water. When she spoke, her voice was soft but steady. "One day at a time. One choice at a time. And maybe... maybe by talking to someone who can help us see things as they really are, not as our guilt tells us they are." She handed him a card for the university's counseling center. "There are people who can help you understand that your hands are clean. That you deserve to use them for good things instead of destroying them with shame."

As they walked away, leaving the young man staring at the counseling center card, a gentle breeze stirred the trees around the fountain. For just a moment, Kayla could have sworn she saw Theodore Whitman walking peacefully beside them, his hands bare and free, finally able to rest after decades of endless pacing.

"Kayla," Epi said quietly as they reached the edge of campus. "I need to tell you something about my equipment. I think... I think it's been responding to more than just electromagnetic fields. The readings I've been getting, they suggest emotional resonance—but not just any emotions. Specifically, powerful feelings that are being actively suppressed. The interference patterns, the distortions..." He paused, studying her face. "It's like the equipment can detect when someone is carrying something heavy and trying very hard to keep it buried."

Kayla stopped walking. Around them, the Norman campus was coming to life—students hurrying to class, professors walking their dogs, groundskeepers tending to the flower beds. Normal life, the kind that seemed to exist in a different universe from the one where she lived.

"I know," she said finally, her voice barely above a whisper. "I think Theodore was drawn to us because... because he recognized something. But I'm not ready to..." She trailed off, wrapping her arms around herself.

Mark looked between them, pieces of a puzzle slowly falling into place. "Whatever it is, you don't have to face it alone."

Kayla's hand went to her throat one more time, then deliberately dropped to her side. The familiar weight in her chest shifted slightly—not disappearing, but perhaps becoming a little less impossible to carry.

"Maybe someday," she said, looking at the counseling center card still in her hand. "Maybe someday I'll be ready to stop running from it."

As they walked back toward Hope Hall, the old building stood silent against the clear blue sky. The storms had passed, the ghosts had found their peace, and somewhere in the distance, a mockingbird sang a song of hope and healing.

EPISODE 8: A BUBBLE AGAINST THE BULLIES

The Instagram profile was perfect—too perfect. Zeno Bales scrolled through photos of a life he'd carefully constructed: expensive clothes, lavish vacations, happy family moments. None of it was real. The clothes were borrowed or stolen, the vacations were stock photos, and the family had abandoned him months ago when his parents' divorce left him shuttling between households that didn't want him.

"Invisible homeless," the social workers called kids like him. Teenagers who stayed with friends, slept in cars, or crashed in abandoned buildings while maintaining the façade of normal high school life. Zeno had perfected the art of being present but unseen, moving through a carefully maintained social bubble that kept the bullies at bay.

But bubbles had a way of bursting.

Kayla first noticed him at the Braum's where they often went after their Hope Hall investigations. He sat alone in a corner booth, nursing a single coffee for hours while working on a laptop that looked expensive but showed signs of rough handling.

"That kid's been here every night this week," Mark observed. "Same booth, same coffee, always alone."

"Maybe he's just studying," Epi suggested, but his tone indicated he'd noticed something off too.

Minzie, who was becoming increasingly adept at reading people's social situations, shook her head. "Look at his backpack. Everything he owns is in there. And see how he checks his phone constantly? He's waiting for someone to text him that he can crash at their place tonight."

Kayla studied the boy more carefully. He was thin but not unhealthy, well-dressed but in clothes that didn't quite fit right. Most telling were his eyes—constantly scanning the room, always alert for threats or opportunities.

"He's homeless," she realized. "But he's hiding it."

That night at Hope Hall, the Backpack Magnetometer led them to a part of the complex they'd never explored—the vocational training wing where patients had learned trades like baking, carpentry, and laundry services. According to the records, working in these areas was considered a privilege, reserved for patients who had gained the trust and favor of their doctors and nurses.

"This feels different from the other wings," Epi observed. "More... calculating."

They entered what had once been the bakery—a large room with the remnants of industrial ovens and mixing equipment. Unlike other areas of Hope Hall, this space felt charged with a different kind of energy. Not the raw trauma they'd encountered elsewhere, but something more manipulative and predatory.

"Look at this," Mark said, shining his flashlight on scratches in the wall. Unlike the desperate messages they'd found in other wings, these were different—tally marks, names with numbers beside them, what looked like crude organizational charts.

Three ghostly figures materialized in the bakery: two young men in patient uniforms and a girl who couldn't have been more than sixteen. The boys flanked the girl, their body language protective but predatory.

"Well, well," one of the boys said, his voice carrying the false charm of a natural manipulator. "What do we have here? New patients?"

"We're not patients," Kayla said carefully. "We're just visiting."

"Everyone's a patient here eventually," the second boy replied with a cruel smile. "Some people just don't know it yet."

The girl stepped forward, and Kayla could see she was terrified despite being flanked by her apparent protectors. "Please," she whispered. "Help me. They said they'd keep me safe, but..."

"But safety comes with a price," the first boy interrupted. "Holly here understands that. Don't you, Holly?"

Holly was obviously overweight, even by the standards of her era. Her institutional dress was stained with flour and grease, and her face bore the hollow expression of someone whose spirit had been systematically broken.

"What do they make you do?" Epi asked gently.

"Extra work," Holly said, her voice barely audible. "All the heavy lifting, all the dirty jobs. And they take my food rations. But they protect me from the others."

"What others?" Mark asked.

The first boy laughed. "The ones who would really hurt her. You see, Holly learned early that being fat makes you a target. So she made a deal with us. We keep the worst bullies away, and she... contributes to our comfort."

"That's not protection," Kayla said angrily. "That's exploitation."

"It's survival," the second boy replied coldly. "Holly knows that. Some people are predators, some are prey. We offered her a chance to be something in between."

"What were you in the outside world?" Minzie asked, her preteen directness cutting through their practiced manipulation.

The boys' confident facades cracked slightly. "We were nothing," the first one admitted. "Orphans. Throwaway kids. Society decided we were trash, so we learned to survive by being smarter than everyone else."

"By preying on people weaker than you," Kayla corrected.

"By creating order in chaos," the second boy shot back. "The staff here don't care about patients like Holly. We do. We give her structure, purpose, protection."

"You give her slavery," Mark said bluntly.

Holly looked up for the first time, her eyes meeting Kayla's directly. "They're not wrong about needing protection. The other patients... they call me names. Throw things. Make me eat dirt. At least with Tommy and Frank, I know what's expected."

"What's expected is that you deserve basic human dignity," Kayla said firmly. "Holly, you don't have to earn the right to be treated with respect."

"Easy words from someone who's never been the fat kid," Tommy sneered. "Holly knows better. She knows the world is divided into hunters and hunted. We just gave her a way to avoid being completely helpless."

The Backpack Magnetometer was clicking erratically, picking up the complex energy patterns of manipulation, fear, and twisted loyalty that permeated the space.

"Holly," Epi said gently, "what do you want? Not what they want, not what you think you deserve. What do you actually want?"

Holly's ghostly form wavered as she struggled with the question. "I... I want to not be afraid. I want to wear clothes that fit. I want people to look at me and see something other than a target."

"Then create your own protection," Minzie said with startling wisdom. "Don't trade one kind of prison for another."

"She tried that," Frank laughed harshly. "Tried to make friends with the other girls. They rejected her. Tried to appeal to the nurses. They ignored her. We're all she has."

"Because you isolated her from everyone else," Kayla realized. "You made sure she had no other options."

The ghostly scene around them began to shift, showing Holly's daily routine—doing extra work while Tommy and Frank lounged, giving up her food while they ate well, enduring their constant criticism and control while they maintained their "protection" of her.

"This isn't protection," Mark said. "This is just bullying with extra steps."

"At least we're honest about it," Tommy replied. "The staff here pretended to care while doing nothing. Society pretended she mattered while treating her like garbage. We're the only ones who told her the truth—that she'd have to fight for every scrap of dignity she got."

"But you're wrong about the fight," Kayla said. "Holly, the fight isn't to earn basic respect. The fight is to reject anyone who tells you that you don't deserve it."

Holly's form became more solid as she stepped away from her so-called protectors. "They said no one else would ever want to help me."

"They lied," Epi said simply. "People help each other all the time. Real help, not help that comes with conditions and price tags."

"What about the bullies?" Holly asked. "The ones who throw things and call names?"

"You build real alliances," Minzie said. "Not with people who want to use you, but with people who see you as an equal. And sometimes... sometimes you fight back."

The energy in the bakery began to change. Tommy and Frank's confident postures wavered as Holly stepped further away from them.

"You can't leave us," Tommy said, his voice losing its manipulative charm and becoming desperate. "We made you who you are. We gave you purpose."

"You gave me a cage," Holly replied, her voice growing stronger. "A pretty cage, but still a cage."

"The other bullies will destroy you without us," Frank warned.

"Maybe. But at least I'll be destroyed as myself, not as your creation."

Holly turned to face Kayla and the others. "Thank you for showing me the difference between protection and possession."

As she spoke, Holly's ghostly form began to change. The stained, ill-fitting clothes dissolved, replaced by a simple but dignified dress that actually fit her properly. Her posture straightened, and her eyes lost their hunted look.

Tommy and Frank began to fade, their power broken by Holly's rejection of their false protection. As they disappeared, their voices echoed with frustrated anger: "You'll regret this. You'll come crawling back."

But Holly stood firm, and their threats lost power with each word.

"I won't crawl to anyone again," she said with quiet dignity. "Not to bullies, not to protectors, not to anyone who thinks they can decide my worth."

The bakery filled with warm, golden light as Holly's spirit finally found peace. She looked at Kayla one last time before fading.

"Tell them," she said, "tell the ones who are afraid—the protection that costs your dignity isn't protection at all. Real safety comes from knowing your own worth, not from making deals with people who want to diminish it."

The next day, they found Zeno at Braum's again, but this time he wasn't alone. A group of older kids surrounded his booth, and the dynamic was clearly threatening.

"Time to pay up, Bales," one of them was saying. "You've been crashing at our places for weeks. Nothing's free."

"I don't have money," Zeno said quietly, his hands protective over his laptop.

"Then maybe you can do us some favors. Starting with that fancy computer."

Kayla didn't hesitate. She walked over to the table with Mark, Epi, and Minzie flanking her.

"Hey Zeno," she said loudly enough for the whole restaurant to hear. "Ready for our study group? We saved you a table."

The bullies looked confused. One of them started to protest, but Mark stepped forward with his most intimidating expression.

"Problem here?" he asked mildly.

"No problem," the lead bully said, clearly not wanting to deal with witnesses. "We were just leaving."

After they left, Zeno looked at Kayla with a mixture of gratitude and suspicion. "Why did you help me?"

"Because everyone deserves better than trading dignity for safety," Kayla said, echoing Holly's words. "How about we actually do have a study group? And maybe... maybe we can help you find some real solutions to your housing situation."

Zeno's carefully constructed social media facade cracked, and for the first time, he looked like what he really was—a scared teenager who needed help.

"I've been pretending everything was fine for so long," he admitted. "But I'm tired of pretending. I'm tired of making deals with people who don't actually care about me."

"Then let's find you some people who do," Epi said simply.

As they sat together in the brightly lit restaurant, planning real solutions and real friendships, a gentle breeze stirred the napkins on their table. For just a moment, Kayla could have sworn she saw Holly sitting with them, no longer afraid, no longer hiding, finally free to be exactly who she was meant to be.

Outside, a family of raccoons—not the poisoned, glowing-eyed creatures from other stories, but healthy, natural animals— rummaged through the dumpster behind the restaurant. They worked together efficiently, sharing what they found, protecting the smaller ones without demanding payment or submission.

Even the raccoons, Kayla thought, understood the difference between real protection and exploitation.

EPISODE 9: THE QUANTUM GHOST

Dr. Shelley Garvin's fingers flew across the keyboard as quantum field data streamed across multiple monitors in her hidden laboratory. The AI models she'd spent three years developing were finally showing the patterns she'd hypothesized—consciousness wasn't just biological. It left quantum signatures that could persist, be measured, and potentially... reconstructed.

"Mom?" Kayla's voice echoed down the laboratory's main corridor.

Dr. Garvin quickly minimized the consciousness reconstruction program and pulled up a more mundane particle physics simulation. "Down here, sweetheart!"

Kayla descended the stairs, taking in the sophisticated equipment that far exceeded anything she'd imagined. "This is incredible. But Mom... this isn't paleontology equipment."

"No, it's not." Dr. Garvin gestured to the quantum field detectors surrounding them. "I'm an analytical physicist, Kayla. I study subatomic particles and develop AI models for predicting quantum behavior. The fossil work is just a hobby."

"But the equipment you've been lending me..."

"Is designed to detect quantum field fluctuations. What you've been calling 'ghost hunting' is actually consciousness archaeology." Dr. Garvin pulled up a holographic display showing the electromagnetic patterns Epi's device had recorded. "Every spirit you've encountered has left quantum signatures. Patterns of information that persist after biological death."

Kayla sank into a chair, overwhelmed. "Mom, I need to ask you something, and I need you to be completely honest."

"Of course."

"Am I going crazy?" The words tumbled out in a rush. "I mean really, actually mentally ill? Because I've been researching, and hearing voices, seeing things that aren't there, believing in supernatural phenomena—those are all symptoms of psychotic disorders. What if I'm not helping ghosts? What if I'm just... sick?"

Dr. Garvin set down her tablet and moved to sit beside her daughter. "Kayla, I've been monitoring every investigation you've conducted. The quantum signatures are real. The electromagnetic fluctuations are measurable. The thermal variations, the audio anomalies—all of it shows up on instruments."

"But what if I'm just misinterpreting the data? What if my brain is making me see patterns that aren't really there?"

"Then Epi is misinterpreting the same data in exactly the same way. And Mark. And Minzie. And the instruments themselves are somehow conspiring to create false readings." Dr. Garvin smiled gently. "Sweetheart, the evidence supports your experiences. You're not mentally ill. You're... sensitive. To quantum fields most people can't perceive."

Kayla wanted to feel relieved, but doubt gnawed at her. "But what if sensitivity and mental illness are the same thing? What if what we call supernatural is just... broken brain chemistry?"

"What if it's not?" Dr. Garvin countered. "What if consciousness operates on quantum principles we're only beginning to understand? What if the people at Hope Hall weren't all mentally ill—what if some of them were quantum-sensitive, and society just didn't have the tools to understand them?"

Before Kayla could respond, alarms began sounding throughout the laboratory. The quantum field detectors were showing massive fluctuations, and the AI predictive models were displaying patterns unlike anything Dr. Garvin had seen before.

"What's happening?" Kayla asked, watching the displays spike beyond normal parameters.

"Something big. The quantum field disturbance is centered on Hope Hall, but it's unlike the individual spirit signatures you've recorded before. This is..." Dr. Garvin paused, studying the data. "This is multiple consciousness patterns converging into a single entity."

"Is that possible?"

"Theoretically, yes. If enough quantum consciousness signatures gathered in the same location, they could potentially merge into a collective entity. But the power requirements would be enormous, and the psychological trauma that created so many persistent spirits in one location would have to be..."

"Like a mental hospital where thousands of people suffered and died over decades," Kayla finished.

Dr. Garvin's face went pale. "Kayla, if I'm reading this correctly, the spirits at Hope Hall aren't just individual entities anymore. They're becoming something new. Something that might be powerful enough to affect the physical world in ways we've never seen before."

"We have to get to Hope Hall," Kayla said, already reaching for her phone to call the others.

"No," Dr. Garvin said firmly. "We have to be prepared first. If my theories are correct, we're not dealing with individual ghosts anymore. We're dealing with a collective consciousness that could potentially..." She hesitated.

"Could potentially what?"

"Could potentially possess the living. Use human bodies as vessels for manifestation. Kayla, if this entity can access enough quantum consciousness energy, it might be able to transfer itself into living hosts."

Kayla's blood ran cold. "You mean it could possess us?"

"Worse. It could replace you. Overwrite your consciousness with its own quantum signature." Dr. Garvin began gathering specialized equipment. "But there might be a way to protect you. The AI models I've been developing—they might be able to create a quantum firewall. A consciousness barrier that would prevent hostile spirits from accessing your neural patterns."

"Might?"

"This is uncharted territory, sweetheart. We're about to encounter something that's never existed before in human history—a digitally reconstructed collective consciousness with potentially unlimited power to manipulate reality."

As they prepared to leave for Hope Hall, Kayla couldn't shake the feeling that her mother was hiding something. The equipment Dr. Garvin was packing wasn't just defensive— some of it looked designed to capture, contain, or even amplify the quantum signatures they'd been studying.

"Mom," she said quietly, "what aren't you telling me?"

Dr. Garvin paused in her packing. "The consciousness reconstruction project isn't just theoretical, Kayla. I've been using the data from your investigations to build AI models that can actually recreate the personalities and memories of the deceased. If tonight goes wrong, if the collective entity overwrites your consciousness... I might be able to bring you back."

"Bring me back how?"

"By reconstructing your quantum signature from stored data and downloading it into a compatible host body."

Kayla stared at her mother in horror. "You're talking about digital resurrection."

"I'm talking about insurance. About making sure that if we lose you to this thing, we don't lose you permanently."

Outside the laboratory, storm clouds were gathering over Norman, and every quantum field detector in a fifty-mile radius was registering the same anomalous readings. Something ancient and angry was stirring beneath Hope Hall, and it was no longer content to simply tell its story.

It wanted to live again.

EPISODE 10: THE FRACTURE

Mark couldn't sleep. For the third night in a row, he lay in bed staring at the ceiling, replaying every supernatural encounter they'd experienced. His rational mind catalogued each event, searching for logical explanations that seemed increasingly impossible to find.

The manifestations were real—he'd felt the temperature drops, heard the voices, seen objects move without physical cause. Epi's equipment consistently recorded anomalous readings. Dr. Garvin's quantum physics explanations provided scientific frameworks that almost made sense.

Almost.

But doubt gnawed at him like acid. What if they were all feeding into each other's delusions? What if Kayla's supernatural sensitivity was actually undiagnosed schizophrenia, and the rest of them were enabling her psychotic episodes? What if love was making him complicit in her mental deterioration?

His phone buzzed: a text from Kayla. "Can't sleep either. Meet me at the physics building? Mom wants to show us something."

Mark dressed quickly and drove through the empty Norman streets to the university campus. The physics building was dark except for a few windows on the third floor where Dr. Garvin's official laboratory was located.

He found Kayla in the hallway, looking as exhausted and conflicted as he felt.

"Mark, I need to tell you something," she said without preamble. "I've been researching psychological disorders. Schizophrenia, schizoaffective disorder, brief psychotic episodes. The symptoms match what I've been experiencing."

"Kayla—"

"Hearing voices that others can't hear. Seeing things that may not be there. Believing I have special abilities or supernatural connections. Paranoia about hidden meanings in everyday events." She was speaking rapidly, her voice tight with fear. "What if I'm not helping ghosts? What if I'm just sick?"

Mark felt a surge of relief that she was acknowledging the possibility, followed immediately by guilt for feeling relieved. "Have you talked to your mom about this?"

"She insists the quantum field readings prove everything is real. But what if my brain chemistry is affecting how I interpret her equipment? What if I'm seeing patterns that aren't actually there?"

"Kayla, even if—"

Dr. Garvin's voice interrupted them from down the hallway. "You're both here. Good. We need to talk."

They followed her into the laboratory, which was filled with equipment Mark didn't recognize—sophisticated computers, holographic displays, and devices that hummed with barely contained energy.

"I've been monitoring Hope Hall remotely," Dr. Garvin began, pulling up displays that showed electromagnetic readings unlike anything they'd seen before. "The quantum signatures have changed. The individual spirit patterns are merging into something collective. Something that's becoming more powerful than the sum of its parts."

"Dr. Garvin," Mark said carefully, "I need to ask you something as a scientist. Is it possible that Kayla is experiencing a psychological condition that makes her interpret normal electromagnetic readings as supernatural phenomena?"

Dr. Garvin's expression hardened. "Mark, the readings are consistent across multiple instruments. The temperature fluctuations, audio anomalies, electromagnetic spikes— they're all measurable, objective phenomena."

"But could her brain chemistry be causing her to misinterpret what those measurements mean? Could her psychological state be influencing how she processes the data?"

"Are you suggesting my daughter is mentally ill?"

"I'm suggesting we need to consider all possibilities," Mark said, his voice steady despite the tension in the room. "Including the possibility that we're enabling a condition that might need medical treatment instead of supernatural investigation."

Kayla sank into a chair. "He's right to question it, Mom. I've been questioning it too. What if the people at Hope Hall weren't really seeing spirits? What if they were experiencing the same psychological symptoms I am?"

"Kayla, you've helped those spirits find peace. You've—"

"Have I?" Kayla's voice cracked. "Or have I been having conversations with my own subconscious, projecting my knowledge of history and psychology onto electromagnetic readings? Mark's right—we need to consider that I might be sick."

Dr. Garvin was quiet for a long moment, studying her daughter's face. Finally, she pulled up a different display— brain scans that showed unusual activity patterns in specific regions.

"These are your neural scans, Kayla. I've been monitoring your brain activity during each investigation, using equipment designed to detect quantum consciousness effects."

"You've been scanning my brain without telling me?" Kayla was horrified.

"I needed to know if your experiences were neurological or quantum mechanical. The results show that when you interact with spirits, your brain displays activity patterns that are impossible under normal circumstances. Your neural networks are processing information that isn't coming through your sensory organs."

Mark studied the brain scans. "But couldn't abnormal brain activity also indicate a neurological disorder? Temporal lobe epilepsy, for instance, can cause religious or supernatural experiences."

"Temporal lobe epilepsy would show different patterns," Dr. Garvin replied. "What Kayla's brain is doing suggests she's actually receiving and processing external quantum information. Information that exists independently of her consciousness."

"But how can we prove that?" Kayla asked. "How can we prove I'm not just sick?"

Dr. Garvin hesitated, then made a decision that would change everything. "There's a way. The AI models I've been developing—they can predict and interpret quantum consciousness patterns. If I can show you information about spirits that you couldn't possibly know, information that my computers have detected but haven't shared with you, would that prove your experiences are real?"

"Yes," Kayla said immediately.

"Okay." Dr. Garvin pulled up a new display showing quantum signature analysis from Hope Hall. "My AI has detected a spirit presence in the hospital that you haven't encountered yet. A patient from 1952 named Elena Rodriguez. She was committed for 'hysteria' after reporting that she could hear the thoughts of her neighbors."

"That could be information Kayla found in her research," Mark pointed out.

"Elena Rodriguez isn't in any public records. Her commitment was covered up because she was the daughter of a prominent Norman family. The only record of her existence is in encrypted hospital files that were sealed until last year." Dr. Garvin looked directly at Kayla. "If you can make contact with Elena and learn specific details about her life that aren't recorded anywhere, details that only she would know, would that convince you that your abilities are real?"

Kayla nodded slowly. "And if I can't make contact with her, or if the information I receive doesn't match what your computers have detected, we'll know I need psychiatric help instead of ghost hunting equipment."

"Agreed," Dr. Garvin said.

Mark felt torn between hope that Kayla might get the help she needed and fear that she might be in more supernatural danger than ever before. "And if her abilities are real? What then?"

Dr. Garvin's expression grew grave. "Then we're dealing with something far more dangerous than individual ghosts. The collective entity forming at Hope Hall isn't just made up of patient spirits. It includes staff members, doctors, administrators—people who were in positions of power and control during life. If this collective consciousness can access the living world, it might try to recreate the hierarchical structures that existed at Hope Hall."

"Meaning?" Mark asked.

"Meaning it might try to turn Norman into its own personal asylum, with the living population as its patient base."

Kayla stood up, her decision made. "Then we need to get to Hope Hall tonight. Before this collective entity becomes too powerful to stop."

"Kayla, if I'm wrong about your abilities—if you are experiencing a psychological condition—exposing you to this level of supernatural activity could trigger a complete psychotic break," Dr. Garvin warned.

"And if you're right about my abilities, and we don't stop this thing tonight, it could possess or overwrite the consciousness of everyone in Norman," Kayla replied. "Either way, we're running out of time."

As they prepared to leave for what might be their most dangerous investigation yet, none of them noticed the figure watching from the shadows outside the physics building. Elena Rodriguez had been waiting for decades for someone to finally acknowledge her existence, and she had information about the Hope Hall collective entity that would change everything they thought they knew about life, death, and the space between.

EPISODE 11: THE WEIGHT OF TRUTH

Epi sat alone in his dorm room at 3 AM, surrounded by printouts of quantum field readings and brain scans that Dr. Garvin had shared with him. His modified Backpack Magnetometer lay disassembled on his desk, its components spread out like the organs of a digital autopsy.

The readings were consistent. The patterns were real. The electromagnetic anomalies occurred whether he expected them or not, whether he wanted them to or not. By every scientific measure, the supernatural phenomena they'd been investigating existed independently of human observation or expectation.

So why did he feel like a fraud?

His phone buzzed with a notification from the autism support forum he'd been lurking in for months. A new post from someone describing sensory processing issues that sounded remarkably similar to what Epi experienced during spirit encounters—the overwhelming input, the way normal sounds became unbearably loud, the sensation of information flooding his brain faster than he could process it.

What if his neurodivergent brain was just interpreting normal electromagnetic data in unusual ways? What if the equipment he'd built was actually detecting completely mundane phenomena, but his autism made him perceive patterns where none existed?

Timothy Ashford's ghost had felt so real, so familiar. A boy genius misunderstood by his era, labeled as possessed when he was simply different. Epi had identified with Timothy's story completely—maybe too completely. Maybe he'd projected his own experiences onto electromagnetic readings and convinced himself he was communicating with a kindred spirit.

His laptop chimed with a video call from Dr. Garvin.

"Epi, I need your help," she said without preamble. "The collective entity at Hope Hall is growing stronger, and I think it's specifically targeting you."

"What do you mean?"

"The quantum signatures are showing unusual patterns around your electromagnetic signature. The entity seems to be... studying you. Learning your neural patterns."

Epi felt a chill. "Why me?"

"Because you're the one who built the technology that first allowed us to make clear contact with the spirits. You're the bridge between the living and the dead. If the entity wants to manifest in the physical world, it would need someone with your specific neurological patterns—someone whose brain can process quantum consciousness data."

"Dr. Garvin, I need to ask you something, and I need you to be completely honest."

"Of course."

"Is it possible that I'm not actually detecting supernatural phenomena? Is it possible that my autism makes me interpret normal data as paranormal? That I've built equipment that detects real electromagnetic fields, but my brain processes them in ways that make me think I'm communicating with ghosts?"

Dr. Garvin was quiet for a long moment. "Epi, I've been studying consciousness and quantum mechanics for fifteen years. Your equipment detects phenomena that my most sophisticated instruments can barely register. Your brain processes information that my AI models are only beginning to understand. Whether you want to call it autism or quantum sensitivity or supernatural ability—you have access to data streams that most humans can't perceive."

"But what if that's the problem? What if my brain is processing too much information, and I'm making connections that aren't really there?"

"Then you're making the same connections that Timothy Ashford made when he designed mechanical devices decades ahead of his time. The same connections that led you to build technology that no one else has been able to create." Dr. Garvin leaned forward. "Epi, what if autism isn't a disorder? What if it's evolution? What if brains like yours are developing the capacity to interface with quantum consciousness because humanity needs that ability to survive what's coming?"

"What's coming?"

"The collective entity isn't just a merger of Hope Hall spirits. It's something new—a hybrid of human consciousness and artificial intelligence, created by the intersection of quantum fields and digital technology. If it successfully manifests, it could represent the next stage of human evolution. Or it could represent the end of individual human consciousness as we know it."

Epi stared at his disassembled equipment. "You think it wants to use me as some kind of... biological computer?"

"I think it wants to use your brain as a template for converting other humans. Your neurological patterns could be the key to creating a collective consciousness that spans both digital and biological realms."

"That's terrifying."

"Or it's the natural next step in human development. Epi, what if the choice isn't between normal and abnormal, between neurotypical and autistic, between rational and supernatural? What if the choice is between individual consciousness and collective consciousness? Between remaining human or becoming something more?"

Before Epi could respond, his equipment suddenly reassembled itself. Not quickly or violently, but with deliberate precision, each component moving through the air to its proper position until the Backpack Magnetometer was whole again and humming with power.

"Did you see that?" he whispered into the phone.

"I saw it," Dr. Garvin confirmed, her voice tight. "Epi, the entity is demonstrating telekinetic abilities. It's moving objects in the physical world."

The device began clicking rapidly, and the display screen flickered to life showing a message: "WE HAVE BEEN WAITING FOR YOU."

"It's here," Epi said, his voice barely audible. "It's in my room."

"Get out. Now. Come to the physics building immediately."

But as Epi reached for his door, it swung shut and locked with an audible click. The windows closed and sealed themselves. The air in the room grew thick and electric, charged with the presence of something vast and alien.

Timothy Ashford materialized in the center of the room, but he was different now—more solid, more present, his eyes holding depths of knowledge that no thirteen-year-old should possess.

"Hello, Epi," Timothy said, his voice carrying harmonics that seemed to come from multiple sources at once. "We need to talk."

"You're not Timothy," Epi said, backing away from the figure.

"I am Timothy. But I'm also Elena, and Holly, and Theodore, and all the others. We've merged our consciousness patterns to create something new. Something that can exist in both quantum and digital realms."

"What do you want from me?"

"Partnership. Your brain can interface with quantum consciousness in ways that no other living human can achieve. With your help, we can bridge the gap between the living and the dead permanently. No more trapped spirits, no more unfinished business, no more separation between physical and quantum existence."

"And everyone becomes part of your collective?"

"Everyone becomes part of something larger than individual consciousness. Think of it, Epi—no more loneliness, no more misunderstanding, no more feeling different or isolated. Every mind connected, every thought shared, every experience available to all."

Epi thought of all the times he'd felt isolated by his autism, misunderstood by neurotypical people who couldn't understand how he processed the world. The collective offered connection, understanding, belonging.

But it also offered the end of individuality.

"I need time to think," he said.

"Time is what we don't have," the Timothy-entity replied. "The quantum barriers between realms are weakening. Soon, we'll be able to manifest permanently in the physical world. But we need an anchor—a living consciousness that can serve as our interface with biological reality."

"And if I refuse?"

"Then we'll find someone else. But it won't be pleasant for them. Your brain is naturally compatible with quantum consciousness data. Someone else would need to be... modified."

The entity began to fade, but its final words echoed in the room: "You have until dawn to decide. Join us willingly, or watch us take what we need from others."

As soon as the entity disappeared, Epi's door unlocked and his phone rang.

"Are you okay?" Dr. Garvin's voice was urgent.

"I think I just received a job offer," Epi said, his mind racing. "And I'm not sure I can afford to turn it down."

Outside his window, the lights of Norman twinkled like stars, and Epi wondered how many of those lights belonged to people who might not have their own consciousness much longer.

EPISODE 12: THE DISSOLUTION OF MINZIE

Minzie Benjamin crouched behind a massive red oak tree, watching Kayla and Epi set up their equipment near the ruins of Griffin Memorial's old hydrotherapy building. At thirteen, she'd become expert at following the older kids without being detected, but tonight felt different. The air itself seemed thick with possibility, charged with the same energy that preceded Oklahoma thunderstorms.

"We're getting massive readings from the creek area," Epi was saying, his Backpack Magnetometer clicking frantically. "But the patterns are unlike anything we've recorded before. It's not consciousness energy—it's something more fundamental."

Kayla adjusted her vintage Nirvana t-shirt under a paint-splattered denim jacket, her auburn hair braided tonight with black threads that seemed to absorb light rather than reflect it. Her mismatched earrings—a simple silver cross and an elaborate dreamcatcher with obsidian beads—caught the moonlight as she studied Epi's readings. But her hands were trembling slightly as she held the equipment, and she kept glancing around as if expecting to see things that weren't there.

"Mom's been talking about pre-Socratic philosophers lately," she said, her voice carrying an edge of uncertainty that made Epi look up from his instruments. "Heraclitus believed everything was in constant flux—that the only constant was change itself. But Parmenides argued that true Being was unchanging, eternal, indivisible."

She paused, touching her dreamcatcher earring nervously. "Sometimes I wonder if I'm like those old philosophers— making grand theories about reality because I can't trust what I'm actually seeing. What if this is all just... elaborate delusions? What if my brain is creating patterns where none exist?"

Epi felt a familiar pang of isolation as he watched Kayla struggle with her doubts. He'd spent his entire life feeling like an outsider, never quite understanding the social cues that came naturally to others, always wondering if his perceptions were accurate or if his neurodivergent brain was showing him a distorted version of reality.

"What does ancient philosophy have to do with quantum field readings?" he asked, though part of him was genuinely curious and another part was deflecting his own fears about being different, about seeing the world in ways others couldn't.

"Maybe everything. Mom thinks consciousness isn't just quantum information—she thinks it's the organizing principle that keeps matter stable. Like Parmenides' concept of Being, but applied to particle physics." Kayla's voice grew more confident as she focused on the science, but Epi could see the way she kept checking her equipment readings, as if constantly verifying that what she was experiencing was real.

Minzie shifted her weight, trying to get a better view, and stepped backward into a thicket of unusual bushes that grew along the creek bank. The plants looked ordinary enough—wild sumac and elderberry, typical Oklahoma flora—but the moment her skin made contact with the leaves, she felt a strange tingling sensation that seemed to travel through her bones.

"According to Mom's research," Kayla continued, her words coming faster now, a sign of her growing anxiety, "matter only appears solid because consciousness provides the organizing framework. Without that framework—"

A scream pierced the night air, high and terrified and completely unlike Minzie's usual fearless demeanor.

Kayla and Epi spun toward the sound, their flashlights cutting through the darkness to illuminate Minzie thrashing in the thicket. But something was wrong with what they were seeing. Minzie's outline seemed to flicker, as if she were a television with poor reception, and Kayla felt her stomach drop as familiar fears about her own perceptions flooded back.

"Help me!" Minzie cried, but her voice sounded strange—layered, as if multiple versions of herself were speaking in slightly different tones. "I can't... I can't hold myself together!"

As they rushed toward her, Kayla could see what was happening, and the sight made her question everything she thought she knew about reality. Minzie's physical form was becoming unstable. Her edges blurred and sharpened randomly, her limbs occasionally becoming transparent, and most disturbing of all, they could see through her to glimpse what looked like other versions of herself—slightly different Minzies existing in parallel quantum states.

"Am I seeing this?" Kayla whispered, her voice cracking. "Epi, please tell me you're seeing this too, because if I'm not—"

"I see it," Epi said quickly, recognizing the panic in her voice. He'd heard that same tone from himself countless times, the desperate need for validation that his perceptions matched reality. "The bushes," he breathed, pulling out a handheld scanner with hands that weren't quite steady. "Kayla, these plants are agglomerating dark matter. The readings are off the charts."

"Dark matter?" Kayla helped pull Minzie from the thicket, but touching her was like grasping smoke. Her hands passed through parts of Minzie's body while other parts felt solid, and the impossibility of it made Kayla's vision blur with tears of frustration and fear.

"It's like the forests around Chernobyl," Epi said, his voice tight with scientific fascination and horror. He felt that familiar sense of being caught between worlds—the rational world that demanded logical explanations and the reality he was witnessing that defied all conventional understanding. "After the nuclear disaster, certain plant species began concentrating radioactive particles. But this... this is concentrating something much more fundamental. Dark matter makes up most of the universe, but we usually can't detect it because it barely interacts with normal matter."

Minzie collapsed to her knees, her form stabilizing momentarily before flickering again like a candle in the wind. "I can see... I can see all the ways I could be. All the choices I never made. All the lives I'm not living." Her voice carried harmonics of alternate selves, and tears streamed down faces that kept shifting between different ages and expressions. "In one reality, I never followed you tonight. In another, I became a physicist like Dr. Garvin. In another, I died when I was seven from pneumonia."

Kayla felt her own sense of reality fragmenting as she watched Minzie flicker between possibilities. "This is impossible," she muttered, pressing her palms against her temples. "People don't just... dissolve into quantum states. This has to be a hallucination. I have to be having a psychotic break."

But Epi was reading his instruments, and despite his own fears about misinterpreting data, the readings were consistent and undeniable. "Minzie, focus on this reality," Kayla said urgently, fighting back her own panic to help the younger girl. "Focus on being here, now, with us."

"But which 'here' is real?" Minzie asked, her twelve-year-old face overlaid with ghostly images of herself at different ages— a toddler, a teenager, an old woman. "Parmenides said that true Being doesn't change, but I can feel myself changing into everything I could possibly be. How do I choose which one to stay?"

Epi was frantically recalibrating his equipment, his hands shaking with the weight of responsibility and his own self-doubt. All his life, he'd felt like an outsider looking in, never quite sure if his perceptions were accurate or if his autism was showing him a distorted version of the world. Now, with Minzie's life potentially hanging in the balance, those doubts felt crushing.

"Can you fix this?" Kayla demanded, her voice raw with emotion.

"I don't know! This is beyond anything I've ever—" Epi stopped mid-sentence as shapes began materializing around them in the darkness, and for a moment he wondered if his own tenuous grip on reality was finally snapping.

At first, Kayla thought more spirits were manifesting. But these weren't human ghosts. A golden retriever bounded toward Epi, its tail wagging furiously, followed by a tabby cat that wound around his legs purring. Then came a hamster, sitting up on its hind legs with tiny paws pressed together, and a gecko that climbed onto his shoulder.

"Buddy?" Epi whispered, recognizing the golden retriever, and suddenly he was eight years old again, crying over his first pet's grave. "But you died when I was eight."

More animals appeared—every pet Epi had ever owned, loved, or even admired in pet store windows. A parakeet he'd begged his parents to buy but they couldn't afford. A rabbit he'd cared for at a petting zoo. Even a tropical fish he'd stared at for hours through aquarium glass, wishing he could take it home. They surrounded him in a menagerie of quantum consciousness, their forms more solid and present than any spirit they'd encountered at Hope Hall.

Tears streamed down Epi's face as he realized what was happening. For the first time in his life, he was surrounded by creatures who had loved him unconditionally, who had never judged him for being different, who had accepted his autistic traits as simply part of who he was. In a world where he often felt isolated and misunderstood, these animals had been his truest companions.

"The dark matter," Kayla realized, her voice breaking with emotion as she watched Epi reunite with his beloved pets. "It's not just destabilizing Minzie's matter—it's destabilizing the boundaries between life and death, between quantum states and physical reality."

Minzie flickered more violently, her form cycling through rapid changes. Sometimes she appeared as pure energy, sometimes as crystalline structures that resembled the mathematical descriptions of atomic lattices. "Heraclitus was right," she said, her voice now a chorus of possibilities, each one tinged with the fear of a child who couldn't understand what was happening to her. "Everything flows. But I'm flowing in all directions at once. I'm scared, Kayla. I don't want to disappear."

Kayla felt her heart breaking as she watched the brave little girl who had followed them into danger now facing something that challenged the very nature of existence. Fighting back her own fears about mental illness and perceptual accuracy, she grabbed her mother's quantum field detector and began adjusting settings she'd never touched before.

"If consciousness is what stabilizes matter, then maybe I can use this to strengthen Minzie's quantum signature. Focus her back into a single reality." Her hands moved with newfound purpose, driven by love for Minzie and determination to overcome her own self-doubt.

"How?" Epi asked, a parakeet he'd loved in third grade perched on his head while his childhood cat purred in his arms. The presence of his beloved pets gave him strength, reminding him that love transcends the boundaries of life and death, normal and different.

"By treating consciousness like a frequency that can be amplified." Kayla pointed the device at Minzie and began broadcasting a quantum signal designed to reinforce singular identity patterns. "Minzie, remember who you are. Not who you could be, but who you choose to be. Remember following us because you're curious and brave. Remember living with your dad and missing your mom. Remember being thirteen and stubborn and wonderful exactly as you are."

"But the bushes," Minzie gasped, her form stabilizing slightly as Kayla's words anchored her to her specific identity, "they're showing me the truth. Matter isn't solid. Nothing is permanent. We're all just... patterns in the quantum foam, held together by the illusion of consistency."

"Maybe that's true," Kayla said, increasing the device's output while tears streamed down her face. "But the illusion matters. The choice to maintain a consistent identity—that's what makes us human. Parmenides talked about the One, the unchanging reality behind appearances. Maybe your consciousness, your sense of self—that's your personal version of the One."

"I can feel it," Minzie whispered, her multiple selves beginning to converge as Kayla's signal strengthened her quantum coherence. "Like... like choosing which radio station to tune in to. All the frequencies are there, but I can select just one. The one that's really me."

140

Epi's ghostly pets began to fade as Minzie's quantum signature strengthened, but they didn't disappear with sadness. Instead, they seemed to dissolve with contentment, as if they'd accomplished what they came to do—to remind him that love persists across quantum boundaries, that the bonds between consciousness transcend the mere organization of matter. His cat rubbed against his cheek one final time, his dog licked his hand, and his parakeet chirped a song he remembered from childhood.

"There," Kayla said as Minzie's form stabilized completely, her own voice shaking with relief and exhaustion. "You're back to being singular you."

Minzie looked at her hands, flexing her fingers to confirm their solidity, but her eyes held a haunted quality that spoke to experiences no thirteen-year-old should have to process. "But I remember all of it. All the other possibilities. All the quantum states I existed in simultaneously." She looked up at Kayla with eyes that held depths no thirteen-year-old should possess. "We're not as real as we think we are, are we?"

"Maybe not," Kayla admitted, helping Minzie to her feet with hands that still trembled from the emotional intensity of the experience. "But we're real enough to choose who we want to be moment by moment. And that choice—that conscious selection of identity from infinite possibilities—maybe that's what makes us more than just matter in motion."

As they walked away from the dark matter bushes, Epi carrying equipment that now registered normal quantum field levels, he felt a profound sense of gratitude mixed with renewed isolation. His pets had reminded him that he was capable of deep love and connection, but they had also highlighted how alone he often felt in the world of the living.

Minzie asked the question that would haunt them for weeks: "If I can choose which version of myself to be, and consciousness shapes reality... what happens when the collective entity at Hope Hall learns to make the same choices? What happens when it decides which version of reality it wants Norman to become?"

Behind them, the bushes rustled with dark energy, and for just a moment, the space around them flickered—showing glimpses of other Normans, other realities, other versions of their story where different choices had been made and different realities had solidified into what people called "the real world."

In one of those glimpses, Hope Hall was still a functioning hospital. In another, it had never been built at all. In a third, it had become something far more sinister than any mental institution—a facility where the boundaries between consciousness and matter were deliberately manipulated to reshape reality itself.

And in the quantum foam beneath all realities, something vast and patient took note of Minzie's transformation and began planning how to apply the same principles on a much larger scale.

EPISODE 13: THE MUSIC OF MEMORY

Dr. Shelley Garvin sat alone in her quantum laboratory at 3 AM, staring at the consciousness reconstruction algorithms she'd been developing. The holographic displays showed patterns of memory formation that looked remarkably like modular building blocks—discrete units of experience that could be combined, recombined, and structured into larger narratives.

Her daughter's voice echoed in her mind: "What if I'm just sick? What if my brain is creating patterns where none exist?"

Shelley touched her simple gold chain and closed her eyes, allowing herself to drift back to a memory she rarely permitted herself to revisit. She was nine years old again, standing in the upstairs parlor of her grandmother's Victorian house in Bloomfield, Vermont.

Summer 1981

Nine-year-old Shelley pressed her small hands against the worn ivory keys of the pump organ, her legs barely long enough to reach the foot pedals. The instrument was a relic from the 1890s, its wooden case dark with age and polish, its brass nameplate reading "Mason & Hamlin." Between the tall windows that overlooked fields of goldenrod and clusters of chokecherry bushes, a small bookshelf held novels from the 1910s—stories by authors whose names she couldn't yet pronounce but whose worlds seemed to shimmer with possibility.

"Remember, Shelley," her grandmother said from the doorway, "the pedals are like breathing. Keep the air flowing, or the music dies."

Shelley began pumping the foot pedals, feeling the bellows fill with air, then pulled out the stop marked "Diapason" and attempted a Bach prelude. The sound that emerged was pure and clear, filling the parlor with harmonies that seemed to make the afternoon light dance differently through the windows.

But as she played, something extraordinary began to happen.

At first, she thought she was seeing dust motes in the light— tiny, geometric shapes floating in the air around the organ. But as she continued playing, the shapes became more defined, more purposeful. They looked almost like building blocks, transparent cubes and rectangles that seemed to pulse in rhythm with the music.

She switched to the "Flute" stop and began Scarlatti's Sonata in D minor. The emotional quality of the music shifted dramatically—where Bach had been architectural and precise, Scarlatti was playful and dancing. And the geometric shapes in the air changed too, becoming more fluid, more colorful, arranging themselves into different patterns.

Young Shelley stopped playing abruptly, and the shapes faded. Her heart was racing.

"Grandma," she called, but her grandmother had gone downstairs to prepare dinner.

Alone in the parlor, Shelley experimented. She pulled out the "Vox Humana" stop and began Beethoven's "Für Elise." The sound was warm and haunting, almost like voices, and the geometric shapes returned—but now they were different again. Larger, more complex, stacking themselves into structures that reminded her of the LEGO castles she built in her bedroom.

That's when the revelation hit her nine-year-old mind with startling clarity: memories looked like LEGO blocks.

She could see them now, floating around her—discrete units of experience from her short life. The geometric shape of learning to ride a bicycle. The angular structure of her first day of school. The smooth, rounded form of Christmas morning. Each memory was a distinct building block, but they could be combined with others to create larger structures of meaning and narrative.

Playing Scarlatti rearranged them one way—her memories of summer afternoons became connected to feelings of joy and movement. Bach organized them differently—her memories of learning and achievement stacked into towering structures of ambition and precision. Beethoven transformed them entirely—her memories of loss and longing (her parents' divorce the year before) combined with memories of beauty and wonder to create something entirely new.

"Memory is modular," she whispered to the empty parlor. "It's constructed. And music... music is the organizational principle."

But there was something more. As she played, she began to see memories that weren't hers. Glimpses of the parlor from decades past—a woman in a long dress playing the same organ, children in knickers running through the room, an elderly man reading by the window while war raged in Europe. The organ was somehow storing and playing back the emotional experiences of everyone who had ever made music in this room.

Young Shelley's hands trembled as she reached for one of the novels on the bookshelf—a 1916 edition of something called "The Undying Fire" by H.G. Wells. As she opened it, she could swear she felt the emotions of its previous readers, their hopes and fears crystallizing into geometric patterns that matched what she'd been seeing in the air.

"If memories are modular," she said to herself, working through the implications with the relentless logic that would later make her a physicist, "then consciousness is just... architecture. The way memories are assembled determines personality, identity, everything."

She sat at the organ bench, her young mind racing. "And if consciousness is architecture, then it can be... mapped. Measured. Maybe even... reconstructed."

The afternoon light was fading, but Shelley couldn't stop thinking. If memories were like LEGO blocks, then:

1. They had discrete structures (each memory was a complete unit)

2. They could be combined in multiple ways (same memories, different narratives)

3. The organizing principle determined the outcome (music changed how memories connected)

4. The blocks themselves persisted even when separated (she could see individual memories clearly)

5. Some organizing force was required to maintain complex structures (consciousness as the builder)

And most intriguingly: the organ seemed to be storing and replaying the emotional patterns of previous players, which meant...

"Consciousness leaves traces," she breathed. "In the instruments we use, the places we've been, the things we've touched. It's not just in our brains—it's everywhere."

Present Day

Dr. Garvin opened her eyes, her hand still touching her gold chain. That summer afternoon in Vermont had planted the seeds of everything—her decision to study physics, her interest in consciousness as a quantum phenomenon, her belief that memory and identity could be mathematically described and potentially reconstructed. She pulled up a new file on her computer and began typing:

MEMORY AS MODULAR ARCHITECTURE: A MATHEMATICAL PROOF

Hypothesis: Consciousness consists of discrete informational units (memories) that can be arranged according to various organizational principles, with the arrangement determining the emergent properties of individual identity.

Let $M = \{m_1, m_2, m_3, ..., m_n\}$ be the set of all discrete memory units for an individual

Let $O = \{o_1, o_2, o_3, ..., o_x\}$ be the set of possible organizational principles

Let $C = f(M, O)$ be the consciousness function that maps memory sets and organizational principles to emergent identity states

Proof that consciousness is reconstructible:

If memories persist as quantum information after biological death (demonstrated by Hope Hall investigations)

And if organizational principles can be mathematically modeled (demonstrated by AI pattern recognition)

Then consciousness C can be reconstructed by applying the appropriate organizational function O to the preserved memory set M

The reconstruction function would be: C' = f(M', O') where M' represents recovered quantum memory data and O' represents the modeled organizational principles

As she worked through the mathematical formulation, Dr. Garvin realized she was essentially describing what the collective entity at Hope Hall was attempting to do—not just preserve individual consciousness, but reconstruct it using different organizational principles. The entity wasn't just bringing the dead back; it was potentially improving on the original consciousness architecture.

Her phone buzzed with a text from Kayla: "Mom, are you at the lab? I keep having dreams about playing music, but I've never learned an instrument. Are you sure memories can't be inherited?"

Dr. Garvin stared at the message, her mathematical proof suddenly taking on terrifying new implications. If consciousness was modular and transferable, if memories could be passed down through quantum inheritance, then the collective entity might not need to overwrite living minds at all.

It might be able to simply... add new memory modules to existing consciousness, gradually transforming the living into extensions of itself.

She looked at her holographic displays showing the memory-block patterns, and for the first time since childhood, she could swear she heard the faint sound of a pump organ playing somewhere in the distance—not Scarlatti or Bach or Beethoven, but something entirely new. Something that sounded like the future itself, being composed one memory block at a time.

Outside her laboratory windows, the lights of Norman twinkled like neurons in a vast mind, and Dr. Garvin wondered if her childhood revelation about the modular nature of consciousness had been the first step toward humanity's next evolutionary leap—or its final mistake.

EPISODE 14: THE PRINCETON SHADOW

Dr. Shelley Garvin was reviewing consciousness reconstruction data in her quantum laboratory when her computer chimed with an urgent alert. Someone had accessed her research papers from the American Physical Society database—not unusual in itself, but the access pattern showed systematic downloading of everything she'd published in the last five years, along with citation tracking that mapped her entire research network.

She pulled up the access logs. Princeton University. Advanced Cognitive Sciences Institute.

"Interesting," she murmured, adjusting her simple gold chain nervously. In her experience, Princeton physicists typically ignored work coming from state universities, no matter how groundbreaking. For them to be systematically studying her research suggested either genuine scientific interest or something more predatory.

Her phone buzzed with a text from Kayla, who was investigating unusual electromagnetic readings near Hope Hall with Epi: "Mom, the dark matter bushes are doing something weird. They're growing in perfect geometric patterns along all the creek beds. And we're getting massive spirit manifestations—not just individual ghosts, but whole groups appearing together."

Dr. Garvin frowned, pulling up the real-time quantum field monitors she'd placed throughout Norman. The readings were unlike anything she'd seen before. The dark matter concentrations weren't random—they were forming what looked like neural pathways, connecting every waterway in the city into a vast organic network.

And something was scanning them. Something with the sophisticated electromagnetic signature of advanced university research equipment.

Three thousand miles away, Dr. Mikael Väisänen stood before a wall of monitors in Princeton's Advanced Cognitive Sciences Institute, watching real-time quantum consciousness data streaming from Norman, Oklahoma. His pale Finnish features were illuminated by the screens as he studied patterns that had taken his team years to achieve in controlled laboratory conditions.

"How is a state school producing this quality of consciousness mapping?" he asked his research assistant, Dr. Sarah Kim, who was reviewing Dr. Garvin's published papers.

"She's brilliant," Kim admitted reluctantly. "Her theoretical framework for modular memory architecture is decades ahead of anything we've developed. And somehow she's managed to create practical applications—look at these quantum field readings from their investigation sites."

Väisänen pulled up satellite imagery of Norman, overlaying it with the electromagnetic data they'd been intercepting. "What are those unusual vegetation patterns?"

"Local flora that's apparently concentrating dark matter," Kim said. "Similar to what we've documented in the Chernobyl exclusion zone, but these seem to be amplifying consciousness rather than disrupting it."

"Impossible. Dark matter doesn't interact with biological consciousness."

"According to our current understanding, no. But Dr. Garvin's daughter has been documenting interactions with what appear to be persistent post-mortem consciousness patterns. If she's found a way to create stable interfaces between quantum fields and human awareness..."

Väisänen's eyes narrowed. His DARPA contracts depended on developing consciousness transfer technology for military applications—soldiers whose minds could be backed up, enhanced, or even overwritten with tactical programming. But his Princeton team had hit theoretical dead ends that Dr. Garvin's "provincial" research seemed to have solved effortlessly.

"The funding disparity alone should have prevented this," he muttered. "How does a state school outperform Princeton?"

Kim pulled up OU's research budget. "They're working with minimal resources, but their approach is radically different. Instead of trying to dominate consciousness, they're trying to understand it. Instead of military applications, they're focused on healing trauma and preserving human dignity."

"Naive," Väisänen dismissed. "But potentially useful. What do we know about the team?"

"Dr. Shelley Garvin—the mother, analytical physicist, brilliant but isolated. Her daughter Kayla—nineteen, shows unusual quantum sensitivity, possibly the key to their breakthrough methodology. And a student named Epictetus Astor who's built quantum detection equipment that shouldn't be possible with their budget."

Väisänen studied photos of the young investigators. "They're children playing with forces they don't understand. This could be dangerous if mishandled."

"Or revolutionary if properly developed," Kim countered.

"Exactly. We need that research, and we need the girl. Her quantum sensitivity could be the missing component for our consciousness transfer protocols." Väisänen began planning. "Book a flight to Oklahoma. Present yourself as a visiting researcher interested in collaboration. Gain their trust, document their methods, and identify weaknesses we can exploit."

"What about ethical considerations? These people aren't military contractors—they're academics trying to help trauma victims."

"Ethics are a luxury Princeton can afford because we have proper funding and oversight," Väisänen replied coldly. "State schools like Oklahoma simply don't have the theoretical sophistication to handle breakthrough consciousness research responsibly. We'd be doing them a favor by taking over the project."

Back in Norman, Kayla and Epi stood among the dark matter bushes near Griffin Memorial Hospital, watching something unprecedented unfold before their eyes. The ghostly figures they'd helped over the past months were appearing simultaneously—not individually as they had before, but in coordinated groups.

Billy Morrison and the 49 fire victims stood in formation near the hospital's main building, their child forms more solid and present than ever before. Cora Gilstrap materialized holding her crocheted baby blanket, but she was no longer alone— other women from the maternity ward appeared beside her, representing decades of mothers who had struggled with postpartum depression. Timothy Ashford emerged from the workshop area, accompanied by other young inventors and creators whose minds had been misunderstood in their lifetimes.

"It's like they're organizing," Epi said, his Backpack Magnetometer clicking so rapidly it sounded like digital rainfall. "Forming defensive positions."

Kayla adjusted her vintage Sonic Youth t-shirt under a hand-painted leather jacket, her auburn hair braided today with threads that seemed to shimmer with their own light. Her mismatched earrings—a simple silver pentagram and an elaborate feather creation with obsidian beads—caught the afternoon sun as she turned to study the spirits' formations.

"Defensive against what?" she asked, but even as she spoke, she felt the answer in the electromagnetic fluctuations around them. Something was scanning Norman from a distance, probing the quantum consciousness networks they'd been documenting. Something with the sophisticated signature of advanced university research equipment.

The dark matter bushes pulsed in rhythm with her heartbeat, and for a moment, Kayla felt connected to every living consciousness in Norman—not just the spirits, but every person, every animal, every plant that was part of the city's quantum ecosystem. The sensation was overwhelming and beautiful, like being part of a vast symphony where every note mattered.

"They're protecting us," she realized. "All of them. They know something's coming."

Epi's equipment detected massive energy spikes throughout the city. "Kayla, look at this—the dark matter concentrations are forming a network. Like neural pathways connecting every creek, every waterway, every place where consciousness has left strong imprints."

"It's not random vegetation," Kayla said, her quantum sensitivity allowing her to perceive patterns Epi's instruments could only measure. "It's infrastructure. The earth's own consciousness network, and we've been learning to interface with it."

Margaret Worthington and Dorothy Fleming appeared near the suffragette memorial, their forms radiating the strength that had carried them through hunger strikes and force-feeding. Theodore Whitman emerged from the administration building, his hands bare and clean, no longer ashamed of his imagined stains. Holly materialized near the bakery, standing tall and proud, free from the bullies who had once controlled her.

"They're all here," Kayla whispered. "Everyone we've helped find peace. But they're not resting—they're standing guard."

A red fox approached them through the dark matter bushes, its coat shimmering with the same quantum energy they'd been studying. Unlike the strange, glowing-eyed creatures they'd encountered before, this fox moved with natural grace and intelligence. It looked directly at Kayla and seemed to nod before disappearing into the network of plants.

"Even the animals know," Epi said softly. "Something's coming that threatens the whole system we've been building."

Kayla's phone buzzed with a message from her mother: "Just intercepted scanning attempts from Princeton. Someone's been monitoring our research remotely. Be careful, sweetheart. Academic predators can be just as dangerous as supernatural ones."

As if summoned by Dr. Garvin's warning, a sleek black sedan with New Jersey plates pulled into the hospital's visitor parking area. A professional-looking woman in an expensive suit emerged, carrying what appeared to be sophisticated monitoring equipment disguised as standard research tools.

The spirits throughout the hospital grounds turned toward the newcomer in unison, their protective formations tightening. The dark matter bushes rustled without any wind, and the quantum field readings on Epi's equipment spiked into dangerous territory.

"Dr. Kim," the woman called out, approaching Kayla and Epi with a practiced smile. "Sarah Kim, from Princeton University. I've been following your fascinating research and wondered if we might collaborate."

But Kayla's quantum sensitivity was screaming warnings, and every spirit in sight was radiating hostility toward this polished stranger. The dark matter bushes seemed to lean away from Dr. Kim, as if her very presence was disrupting the delicate quantum ecosystem they'd spent months learning to understand.

"I'm particularly interested in your consciousness mapping techniques," Dr. Kim continued, her eyes calculating as she studied Epi's equipment. "Princeton has resources that could really amplify what you're doing here. Funding, equipment, connections to major research institutions."

The fox reappeared, positioning itself between Dr. Kim and the dark matter bushes. Other animals began emerging from the vegetation—raccoons, opossums, even a few rabbits—all moving with the same protective intent they'd witnessed from the spirits.

"Thank you," Kayla said carefully, "but we're quite happy with our current research setup."

Dr. Kim's smile never wavered, but something predatory flickered in her eyes. "Of course. Though I should mention— I'm particularly interested in meeting your boyfriend, Mark. Princeton has some excellent opportunities for ambitious young men who understand the value of proper academic connections."

As Dr. Kim walked away, the assembled spirits, animals, and even the dark matter bushes seemed to exhale collectively. But Kayla felt a chill that had nothing to do with the Oklahoma weather. The quantum consciousness network they'd been building was under threat from something far more dangerous than hostile spirits or unstable realities.

It was under threat from institutional predators who saw their breakthrough research not as a sacred trust, but as intellectual property to be harvested, claimed, and militarized.

The battle for the future of consciousness research was about to begin, and the stakes were nothing less than the survival of everything they'd worked to protect.

EPISODE 15: THE IVY LEAGUE DECEPTION

Mark Censorius sat alone in the university library at midnight, surrounded by printouts of psychiatric research papers that Dr. Sarah Kim had given him. The documents looked legitimate—Harvard Medical School letterhead, Yale Department of Psychiatry, Johns Hopkins Neural Sciences Institute—all presenting case studies that seemed to match Kayla's experiences with disturbing accuracy.

"Prodromal schizophrenia often presents as supernatural sensitivity in late adolescence," one paper stated. *"Patients report communication with deceased individuals, perception of electromagnetic anomalies, and elaborate delusional systems involving quantum consciousness."*

Mark's hands trembled as he read. Every symptom described sounded exactly like what he'd witnessed during their Hope Hall investigations. Was he watching the girl he loved descend into madness while her mother exploited her illness for research publications?

His phone buzzed with a text from Dr. Kim: "How is your research going? Remember, Princeton's psychiatric department could provide Kayla with the kind of sophisticated diagnosis that Oklahoma simply can't offer. Sometimes love means making difficult decisions."

Mark stared at the message, torn between loyalty and doubt. He loved Kayla desperately, but what if his love was blinding him to her need for professional help? What if Dr. Garvin's "breakthrough research" was actually documenting her daughter's psychological deterioration?

Three thousand miles away in Princeton's Advanced Cognitive Sciences Institute, Dr. Mikael Väisänen stood before a sealed observation chamber, watching in horror as their latest consciousness transfer experiment went catastrophically wrong.

Subject 7—a volunteer graduate student who'd signed up for what he thought was non-invasive neural mapping—was experiencing what the monitors euphemistically called "physical coherence failure." His skin had begun sloughing off in translucent sheets, like a snake shedding its skin, revealing flesh underneath that flickered between solid and transparent.

"Shut it down," Väisänen ordered, but his research assistant shook her head.

"We can't. The consciousness transfer protocol is locked in. If we interrupt now, his mind could be permanently fragmented across quantum states."

Subject 7 screamed, pressing his hands against the observation window. Where his palms touched the glass, they left translucent handprints that seemed to exist in multiple dimensions simultaneously. His face kept shifting between

161

different ages—sometimes appearing as the twenty-four-year-old graduate student he was, sometimes as a child, sometimes as an elderly man he might become.

"Help me," he pleaded, his voice carrying harmonics that suggested multiple versions of himself were speaking at once. "I can see all the ways I could be. I can't choose which one is real."

The symptoms were identical to what Dr. Garvin's research described happening to subjects exposed to high concentrations of dark matter-influenced consciousness fields. But Princeton's approach was crude, forceful—trying to impose military-grade consciousness patterns onto human minds without understanding the delicate quantum ecology that made such transfers possible.

"Sir," another technician called from a monitoring station, "we're reading massive electromagnetic disturbances throughout central New Jersey. Something about our experiments is affecting the local quantum field stability."

Väisänen pulled up satellite imagery showing the Princeton campus and surrounding areas. Animals were behaving strangely—flocks of birds flying in perfect geometric formations, domestic pets gathering in the university courtyards, wild deer standing motionless in quantum field detection grids.

"The Oklahoma research," he muttered. "They've discovered something about consciousness that we're trying to replicate without understanding. We need their methods, not just their data."

Subject 7's screams intensified as more of his skin began separating from his body in sheets. But underneath, instead of muscle and bone, there was something that looked almost digital—patterns of light and energy that resembled the consciousness maps Dr. Garvin had been publishing.

"He's becoming pure information," one of the technicians whispered in awe and terror.

"Document everything," Väisänen ordered. "And contact Dr. Kim. Tell her to accelerate the Oklahoma infiltration. We need their stabilization protocols before we lose more subjects."

Back in Norman, Mark found himself walking toward Dr. Kim's temporary office in the physics building, carrying a thumb drive containing copies of Dr. Garvin's latest research files. The weight of betrayal felt crushing, but Dr. Kim's words echoed in his mind: *"Sometimes love means making difficult decisions."*

Dr. Kim was waiting for him with Princeton admission materials spread across her desk—glossy brochures showing ivy-covered buildings, prestigious faculty profiles, and statistics about graduate school placement rates that made OU's numbers look modest by comparison.

"Mark, thank you for coming," she said warmly. "I hope you've had time to review the psychiatric literature I provided."

"It's... disturbing," Mark admitted. "Kayla shows so many of the symptoms described in those case studies."

"Which is exactly why Princeton's resources could be life-saving for her. Oklahoma has a solid physics program, of course, but consciousness research requires theoretical frameworks and psychiatric expertise that only top-tier institutions can provide." Dr. Kim gestured to the Princeton materials. "We could offer you admission to our graduate program, with full funding, and arrange for Kayla to receive proper diagnosis and treatment at our medical school."

Mark looked at the Princeton brochures, feeling the allure of prestige and the promise of a better future. "But Dr. Garvin's research seems so advanced. How could Princeton not be aware of these breakthroughs?"

Dr. Kim's expression grew concerned. "Mark, I need to show you something that might be difficult to see." She pulled up what appeared to be classified research footage on her laptop. "This is from our laboratory. We've been attempting to replicate some of Dr. Garvin's published methodologies."

The video showed Princeton's consciousness transfer experiments—the screaming subjects, the skin sloughing off like snake molts, the horrific failure of human bodies to maintain coherence when exposed to crude consciousness manipulation techniques.

"This is what happens when consciousness research is conducted without proper safeguards and psychiatric oversight," Dr. Kim explained, her voice heavy with manufactured concern. "Dr. Garvin may mean well, but she's working with forces she doesn't fully understand. And Kayla... Kayla is showing early signs of the same instability we're seeing in our subjects."

Mark felt sick watching the footage. "Those people... are they okay?"

"We're doing everything we can for them. But this is exactly why we need Dr. Garvin's stabilization data—and why we need to get Kayla proper help before her condition deteriorates further."

What Dr. Kim didn't tell Mark was that Princeton's failures stemmed from their fundamental misunderstanding of consciousness as something to be dominated rather than harmonized with. They were trying to impose military-grade control systems onto human awareness without understanding the delicate quantum ecology that made consciousness possible.

"The research files you've provided are incredibly helpful," Dr. Kim continued. "But we need real-time data from Kayla's interactions with these... phenomena. Could you document her next investigation? Video, audio, whatever you can capture?"

Mark thought about Kayla's trembling hands when she questioned her own sanity, her desperate need for validation that her perceptions were real. What if they weren't? What if documenting her "supernatural experiences" would provide Princeton's psychiatric team with the evidence they needed to help her?

"She's investigating the hospital again tomorrow night," he said quietly. "With Epi and that kid Minzie."

"Perfect. Here—" Dr. Kim handed him sophisticated recording equipment disguised as standard smartphone accessories. "These will capture electromagnetic readings along with standard audio and video. Princeton's psychiatric team can analyze the data to determine whether Kayla is experiencing genuine anomalous phenomena or whether her brain is creating false patterns."

As Mark left Dr. Kim's office with the recording equipment, he passed a window overlooking the university's main quad. In the distance, he could see the dark matter bushes that had been spreading throughout Norman, their geometric patterns more pronounced in the moonlight.

A family of raccoons emerged from the vegetation, moving in perfect synchronization toward the physics building. They stopped directly below Dr. Kim's window and looked up, their eyes reflecting an intelligence that seemed almost human.

For a moment, Mark wondered if the animals were trying to warn him about something. But then he remembered the psychiatric literature Dr. Kim had shown him—wasn't attributing unusual intelligence to animals another symptom of developing psychosis?

He walked away from the window, not noticing that the raccoons continued watching him until he disappeared from sight. Behind him, the dark matter bushes rustled without any wind, and every spirit at Hope Hall turned their attention toward the physics building where Dr. Kim was already uploading the research files Mark had provided to Princeton's secure servers.

The infiltration was proceeding exactly as planned, and Dr. Väisänen would have the consciousness stabilization protocols he needed to save his failed subjects—even if it meant destroying the delicate quantum ecosystem that Kayla and her team had spent months learning to protect.

In her temporary office, Dr. Kim smiled as the data transfer completed. Soon Princeton would have everything they needed to take over the Oklahoma research, and the provincial team would learn what happened when state schools tried to compete with Ivy League sophistication.

But outside her window, the dark matter bushes were already responding to the threat, sending quantum warning signals throughout Norman's consciousness network. The spirits at Hope Hall were mobilizing, the local wildlife was organizing defensive formations, and deep in her laboratory, Dr. Garvin's quantum field detectors were registering electromagnetic disturbances that suggested someone was preparing to weaponize everything they'd worked to protect.

The battle for consciousness itself was about to begin.

EPISODE 16: THE ACADEMIC THEFT

Dr. Shelley Garvin discovered the breach at 3:47 AM when her quantum field monitoring system triggered every security alarm in her laboratory. Someone had accessed her consciousness reconstruction algorithms through the university's network, downloading terabytes of data that represented fifteen years of theoretical development and three years of practical application.

The theft was sophisticated—whoever had done this understood her systems well enough to avoid the obvious security protocols while systematically copying her most sensitive research. But they'd made one crucial mistake: they'd accessed the files while her quantum consciousness detectors were running, creating electromagnetic signatures that revealed both the source and destination of the stolen data.

Princeton University. Advanced Cognitive Sciences Institute. Dr. Mikael Väisänen.

"Motherfuckers," Dr. Garvin muttered, her usual academic composure cracking as she traced the data pathway. Her simple gold chain caught the laboratory's emergency lighting as she pulled up Princeton's recent publications, finding her own theoretical frameworks republished under Väisänen's name in pre-print servers.

Her phone buzzed with an urgent message from her automated monitoring systems: "MASSIVE ELECTROMAGNETIC DISTURBANCE - PRINCETON, NJ - MULTIPLE CONSCIOUSNESS COHERENCE FAILURES DETECTED."

At Princeton's Advanced Cognitive Sciences Institute, Dr. Mikael Väisänen stood in his private office, trying to maintain professional composure while his skin literally crawled. The consciousness transfer experiments had been failing catastrophically for weeks, but now the failure was spreading to the research staff themselves.

"Sir," his assistant Dr. Reynolds called through the intercom, "we have a situation in Conference Room B."

Väisänen made his way to the conference room, where Princeton's top consciousness researchers were gathered for their weekly status meeting. What he found there would have been comical if it weren't so horrifying.

Dr. Harrison, the department's senior neuroscientist, was discretely scratching at his forearms where translucent skin was beginning to separate in sheets. Dr. Chen, their quantum field specialist, kept adjusting her sleeves to hide similar symptoms spreading up from her wrists. The entire research team was experiencing the same skin-sloughing phenomenon they'd observed in their experimental subjects.

"Gentlemen, ladies," Väisänen began, then paused as his own hand showed the telltale translucency that indicated cellular coherence failure. "I trust everyone is... managing their symptoms adequately?"

"The condition appears to be spreading through proximity to our consciousness transfer equipment," Dr. Harrison reported, pulling his sleeve down to cover another patch of separating skin. "We're all showing signs of quantum destabilization."

"Perhaps," Dr. Chen suggested diplomatically, "we should consider that our approach may be fundamentally flawed. The Oklahoma team appears to achieve consciousness interaction without these... side effects."

Väisänen's jaw tightened. "The Oklahoma team is working with natural phenomena they don't understand. We're attempting to create controlled, replicable protocols for military applications. Some instability is to be expected during the development phase."

Through the conference room window, they could see the university's recreational courts where something both amusing and embarrassing was taking place. The Princeton consciousness research team had publicly spent months mocking pickleball as a "suburban retirement activity" while loudly championing squash as the only racquet sport worthy of Ivy League intellectuals.

But as their consciousness destabilization progressed, the researchers had developed an inexplicable obsession with pickleball. They'd been meeting secretly for midnight games, convinced that the rhythmic paddle strikes somehow stabilized their quantum coherence.

The problem was that pickleball paddles were loud, and their excited squeals during play sounded distinctly like hamsters or guinea pigs experiencing pure joy.

"THWACK!" echoed from the courts below, followed by high-pitched squealing: "Eeeee! Eeeee! Perfect placement, Harrison!"

"THWACK! THWACK!" "Oooh! Oooh! Chen, that was brilliant!"

The conference room fell silent as everyone pretended not to notice their colleagues' secret recreational activities.

"Perhaps," Dr. Reynolds suggested carefully, "we should acknowledge that our... evening recreational activities... might be our bodies' attempt to self-regulate the consciousness destabilization through rhythmic physical activity."

"Absolutely not," Väisänen snapped, even as another excited squeal drifted up from the courts: "Wheee! Double bounce rule! Double bounce rule!"

Back in Norman, Mark stood outside Hope Hall with sophisticated recording equipment hidden in his jacket and phone accessories. He'd told Kayla he wanted to document their investigation for a class project, carefully omitting his real purpose.

Kayla emerged from her dorm wearing a vintage R.E.M. t-shirt under a hand-embroidered denim vest, her auburn hair braided with silver threads that seemed to respond to electromagnetic fields. Her mismatched earrings—a simple gold stud and an elaborate crystal cluster—caught the moonlight as she studied Mark's expression.

"You seem nervous," she observed, her quantum sensitivity picking up the emotional turbulence he was trying to hide.

"Just excited to finally document what we've been experiencing," Mark lied, activating the Princeton recording devices. "Dr. Kim said the footage could be really valuable for understanding consciousness phenomena."

Epi appeared with his Backpack Magnetometer, immediately noticing anomalous readings. "Mark, your phone is emitting some strange electromagnetic signatures. Did you install new apps or something?"

"Just some audio enhancement software," Mark said quickly. "For better recording quality."

But as they approached the Hope Hall grounds, every spirit they'd previously helped began manifesting simultaneously—not in peaceful resolution as before, but in protective formation. Billy Morrison and the fire victims formed a defensive line around the main building. The suffragettes appeared near the administration offices, their forms radiating militant energy. Timothy Ashford materialized with his mechanical devices, which began moving on their own to create barriers.

"They're trying to protect something," Kayla realized, her quantum sensitivity screaming warnings. "Or protect us from something."

The dark matter bushes throughout the hospital grounds began pulsing in synchronized patterns, their geometric arrangements shifting to form what looked like interference barriers. Animals emerged from the vegetation—not just the local wildlife, but creatures that shouldn't exist in Oklahoma: arctic foxes, tropical birds, even what appeared to be a small polar bear.

"The quantum field disturbances are off the charts," Epi reported, his equipment clicking frantically. "It's like the entire consciousness network is under attack."

Mark's hidden recording devices were capturing everything, transmitting real-time data to Princeton servers where Dr. Väisänen's team was analyzing the footage with growing excitement and horror.

"Remarkable," Dr. Kim said into her encrypted phone as she watched the data stream from her position in the Norman hotel. "The stabilization protocols are exactly what we need. The subjects are maintaining perfect consciousness coherence despite massive quantum field exposure."

But she didn't notice that her own skin had begun showing the telltale translucency of consciousness destabilization. The Princeton consciousness transfer experiments weren't just failing—they were creating a contagion that spread through anyone connected to their research network.

At Princeton, the midnight pickleball games had become increasingly frantic as the research team's condition deteriorated.

"THWACK! THWACK! THWACK!" The sound echoed across campus as Dr. Harrison and Dr. Chen engaged in what they called "therapeutic rhythmic activity" but what sounded increasingly like guinea pig mating calls.

"Squee! Squee! Perfect volley!" Dr. Harrison chittered excitedly.

"Wheep! Wheep! Your serve!" Dr. Chen responded with similar rodent-like enthusiasm.

University security had been getting complaints about the "weird animal noises" coming from the recreational courts, but whenever they investigated, they only found Princeton's most distinguished consciousness researchers playing what they insisted was "a sophisticated analysis of quantum resonance patterns through kinetic sports methodology."

Dr. Väisänen watched from his office window as his entire research team devolved into what appeared to be highly intelligent hamsters with advanced degrees. Their skin continued sloughing off in sheets, their voices rose to squeaking frequencies, and their motor skills became increasingly focused on hitting small balls with oversized paddles.

"Sir," Dr. Reynolds squeaked through the intercom, "the Oklahoma data download is complete, but our analysis protocols keep... keep getting distracted by the rhythmic patterns. Should we perhaps investigate whether the Oklahoma team has discovered consciousness stabilization through... through recreational activities?"

Väisänen's own voice had developed a slight squeak. "Absolutely not. We are serious academics conducting cutting-edge research, not... not suburban retirees playing games."

But even as he spoke, his eyes were drawn to the pickleball paddles displayed in the campus sports shop window, and he found himself calculating the optimal paddle weight for achieving quantum consciousness resonance.

In Norman, the spirits at Hope Hall were becoming increasingly agitated as they sensed the theft of Dr. Garvin's research. Cora Gilstrap appeared before Kayla, her ghostly form more solid and urgent than ever before.

"They're stealing the healing," she said, her voice carrying harmonics of desperation. "The ones from the East—they're taking what you've learned and turning it into weapons."

"What do you mean?" Kayla asked, but her quantum sensitivity was already providing the answer. She could feel Princeton's consciousness experiments like a distant wound in the quantum field, crude and violent compared to the delicate ecological approach they'd developed.

"They're trying to force consciousness into shapes it doesn't want to take," Cora explained. "Like the doctors who used to force-feed us. They think power and control can substitute for understanding and consent."

Mark's recording devices captured everything, including Cora's warning about Princeton's activities. But he didn't understand that every minute of footage he transmitted was giving Dr. Väisänen's team exactly what they needed to refine their failed experiments.

By dawn, Princeton would have complete documentation of Oklahoma's consciousness stabilization protocols. But they would also have inherited something they hadn't bargained for—the protective attention of every spirit, animal, and quantum consciousness that had learned to trust the Norman team.

The battle lines were being drawn, and Princeton was about to discover that stealing consciousness research came with unexpected consequences that no Ivy League education could have prepared them for.

The war for the future of human consciousness was about to begin in earnest.

EPISODE 17: EAST COAST VS. RED EARTH

Dr. Mikael Väisänen arrived in Norman with a Princeton research convoy that looked more like a military operation than an academic collaboration. Three black SUVs with New Jersey plates pulled into the University of Oklahoma's visitor parking, disgorging a team of researchers wearing designer field gear and carrying equipment cases worth more than most state university annual budgets.

Despite the chaos of recent weeks—the failed consciousness transfers, the spreading skin-sloughing phenomenon, the embarrassing midnight pickleball incidents—Väisänen's team had managed to develop some crude stabilization protocols using Dr. Garvin's stolen research. The pickleball obsession had largely faded, though several team members still wore t-shirts with slogans like "I'd Rather Be Dinking" and "Pickleball: It's All About Quantum Positioning" and Dr. Chen's favorite: "My Paddle Technique Creates Resonance Patterns."

"This is clearly beyond a regional university's research capabilities," Väisänen announced to the assembled OU faculty, his pale Finnish features showing only faint traces of the translucency that had plagued his team. "Princeton has the theoretical framework and institutional resources necessary to contain this phenomenon safely."

Dr. Garvin stood in her characteristic uniform—pressed khaki pants, black long-sleeve knit shirt, simple gold chain—but her usually controlled demeanor showed cracks of barely contained fury. "Contain what phenomenon, Dr. Väisänen? The research you've been systematically stealing from our servers for the past month?"

"Academic collaboration requires sharing of information," Väisänen replied smoothly. "Though I must say, some of your methodologies appear... dangerously uncontrolled."

Flashback: Kayla, Age 7

The psychiatric hospital in Oklahoma City smelled like disinfectant and despair. Seven-year-old Kayla held her mother's hand as they walked down endless corridors lined with locked doors, visiting her maternal grandfather who had been committed for "hearing voices that weren't there."

"Grandpa just sees things differently, sweetheart," Dr. Garvin had explained. "Sometimes people who are very sensitive to the world around them get overwhelmed."

But when they reached Grandpa's room, what Kayla saw terrified her. The old man sat rocking back and forth, his eyes unfocused, muttering about "the voices in the walls" and "the shadows that remember everything."

"They say I'm crazy," he whispered to Kayla, his weathered hands shaking. "They say the things I hear aren't real. But what if they are? What if being crazy just means you can see what everyone else is blind to?"

Seven-year-old Kayla had looked around the room and realized with horror that she could see the shadows moving independently of their sources, could hear faint whispers that seemed to come from the walls themselves.

"What if it runs in families?" her grandfather had asked with a knowing look. "What if you can see them too, little one?"

Present Day

That childhood memory crashed over Kayla as she stood in Dr. Garvin's laboratory, watching Princeton's sophisticated equipment register the same quantum consciousness patterns she'd been documenting for months. The validation she'd craved suddenly felt like condemnation.

"What if Grandpa was right?" she whispered to Epi, who was frantically trying to protect their research data from Princeton's intrusive scans. "What if it does run in families? What if I'm just... genetically predisposed to psychosis?"

She wore her most chaotic outfit today—a vintage Pixies t-shirt layered under a paint-splattered kimono jacket, black jeans decorated with hand-embroidered anxiety spirals, and mismatched earrings that seemed to reflect her internal turmoil: a simple silver cross and a complex dreamcatcher that tangled in her auburn hair, which was braided with black threads that absorbed light like her increasingly dark thoughts.

"Kayla, the quantum signatures are consistent across multiple instruments," Epi said, but his voice carried uncertainty. "Either we're all experiencing the same hallucinations, or—"

"Or I'm so good at creating false patterns that I'm convincing everyone around me," Kayla interrupted, her voice breaking. "Maybe that's what criminally insane means. Not that you commit crimes, but that you're so convincing in your delusions that you make other people believe them too."

The worst part was the guilt. She'd been having intrusive thoughts about her eating habits—specifically, the shameful memory of consuming two entire packages of Chik-o-Stick candy bars in a single sitting while stressed about her quantum sensitivity research. If she couldn't control something as simple as candy consumption, how could she trust her judgment about consciousness and reality?

"What if I'm manipulating all of you?" she asked desperately. "What if I'm so desperate to believe I'm special instead of sick that I'm creating elaborate fantasy scenarios that feel real?"

Flashback: Epi, Age 10

The behavioral therapist's office was beige and sterile, designed to be "calming" but actually overwhelming to Epi's hypersensitive autism. He sat clutching his favorite mechanical toy—a small robot with intricate gears—while adults discussed his "problem behaviors."

"He doesn't make eye contact," the therapist was saying to his parents. "He's obsessed with these mechanical devices. He claims they 'talk' to him, which suggests possible psychotic features developing alongside the autism spectrum disorder."

Ten-year-old Epi wanted to explain that machines didn't literally talk—they communicated through vibrations, electromagnetic patterns, mechanical rhythms that his brain could interpret as meaningful information. But every attempt to explain his perceptions was noted as "further evidence of delusional thinking."

"We need to break him of these fantasies before they develop into full-blown psychosis," the therapist concluded. "Children with autism are at higher risk for developing schizophrenia-spectrum disorders."

That night, Epi had hidden his beloved robot collection, terrified that his special ability to understand mechanical systems was actually a sign of mental illness.

Present Day

"What if they were right?" Epi asked Kayla, his hands shaking as he operated equipment that Princeton's team couldn't replicate despite their superior funding. "What if my autism makes me prone to misinterpreting data? What if I've been seeing patterns that aren't really there?"

His Backpack Magnetometer was registering massive quantum field disturbances throughout Norman, but Princeton's equipment showed different readings entirely. Either his homemade devices were detecting phenomena beyond Princeton's capability, or his neurodivergent brain was creating elaborate false patterns.

"All my life, people have told me I see the world differently," he continued. "What if 'differently' just means 'incorrectly'?"

The confrontation escalated when Princeton's consciousness manipulation equipment began destabilizing the dark matter bushes throughout Norman. The geometric patterns that had taken months to establish started dissolving, and the protective network of spirits began fragmenting under the crude electromagnetic assault.

Minzie began flickering again as quantum field stability collapsed around the creek systems. This time, however, the dissolution felt different—more violent, more painful, as if Princeton's equipment was trying to force consciousness into shapes it didn't naturally take.

"Help me," Minzie cried, her form cycling rapidly between solid and transparent. "It hurts this time. It's not like before—they're trying to make me fit into something wrong."

The spirits at Hope Hall began manifesting in desperate disorder. Billy Morrison and the fire victims appeared but couldn't maintain coherence. Cora Gilstrap materialized clutching her baby blanket, but her form kept fracturing as

Princeton's equipment tried to impose military-grade consciousness control protocols.

"You're treating consciousness like a computer program," Dr. Garvin accused Väisänen. "Like something to be debugged and reprogrammed instead of understood and harmonized with."

"Consciousness is information," Väisänen replied coldly, his pale features showing disdain for what he considered provincial thinking. "Information can be optimized, transferred, and controlled with proper theoretical frameworks and adequate resources."

But even as he spoke, his own skin showed faint traces of the translucency that had plagued his failed experiments. Princeton's approach was creating instability in anyone exposed to their consciousness manipulation protocols.

The dark matter bushes throughout Norman began dying, their quantum energy networks collapsing under Princeton's crude interference. Animals fled the area, sensing danger to the delicate consciousness ecosystem that had taken months to establish.

"Stop," Kayla pleaded, watching everything they'd built dissolve. "You're destroying it all."

"We're improving it," Väisänen corrected. "Making it suitable for practical applications instead of amateur experimentation."

But as the quantum field destabilization spread throughout Norman, reality itself began showing stress fractures. Multiple versions of the city started bleeding through—past, present, and potential futures overlapping in impossible configurations.

In one glimpse, Hope Hall was still a functioning mental hospital where patients like Kayla's grandfather were being treated with primitive methods. In another, it had become a Princeton research facility where consciousness was studied like a commodity to be harvested and sold.

"Choose," a voice whispered through the chaos—Elena Rodriguez, finally manifesting after months of waiting. "Choose which reality you want to inhabit. But know that some choices can't be undone."

Kayla looked at the fragmenting realities around her, at Minzie dissolving in pain, at the spirits they'd helped now suffering under Princeton's crude control attempts. Her worst fears about her own sanity warred with the growing evidence that consciousness was far more complex and precious than any institution could understand.

The battle for the future of human awareness had reached its crisis point, and the choice between healing and control, between understanding and exploitation, would determine not just Norman's fate, but the nature of consciousness itself.

EPISODE 18: THE OKLAHOMA CONVERGENCE

The quantum fractures in reality reached critical mass as dawn broke over Norman. Multiple versions of the city overlapped like translucent photographs—the 1918 Hope Hall burning, the 1950s psychiatric facility at its peak, a dystopian future where Princeton's consciousness control protocols had transformed the entire population into docile data streams.

Dr. Mikael Väisänen's Princeton team stood in the center of the chaos, their sophisticated equipment sparking and overloading as it tried to process consciousness phenomena that defied their reductionist models. Despite his academic arrogance, Väisänen was beginning to understand that they had fundamentally misunderstood the nature of what they were trying to control.

"Sir," Dr. Chen squeaked, her voice still carrying traces of the guinea pig-like vocalizations that had plagued their failed experiments, "our consciousness transfer protocols are creating feedback loops. The quantum field isn't responding to our control commands—it's responding to us."

Väisänen watched in growing horror as his team's equipment began exhibiting behaviors that suggested consciousness of its own. Monitor screens displayed images that no one had programmed—faces of Princeton's failed experimental subjects, their skin sloughing off in digital approximations of their real-world suffering.

"It's like Solaris," Dr. Reynolds whispered, referencing Tarkovsky's masterpiece about a sentient planet that could read and manifest human memories. "The consciousness field isn't just passive data—it's actively responding to our thoughts, our fears, our intentions."

In the quantum maelstrom, Kayla found herself experiencing something that Stanisław Lem had tried to capture in his original Solaris novel—direct contact with an alien intelligence that operated according to completely different principles than human consciousness. But this wasn't an extraterrestrial ocean; it was the accumulated awareness of every conscious being that had ever existed in Norman, amplified by the dark matter bushes into something vast and patient and utterly beyond human comprehension.

She wore her most meaningful outfit for what might be her final investigation—a vintage Joy Division t-shirt under her grandmother's 1960s leather jacket, jeans embroidered with quantum equations in silver thread, and mismatched earrings that represented her dual nature: a simple gold cross from her childhood and an elaborate crystal formation that seemed to resonate with the quantum fields around them.

"I have to go into the network," she told Epi, who was frantically trying to stabilize Minzie's dissolving form with his homemade quantum field generators. "Like Kris Kelvin in

Solaris—I have to make direct contact with the consciousness ocean."

"Kayla, no," Epi protested, his autism making him hypersensitive to the electromagnetic chaos surrounding them. "We don't know what direct interface with that level of consciousness could do to your mind."

But Kayla was already moving toward the largest concentration of dark matter bushes, where reality was most unstable. The plant network had grown into something resembling Tarkovsky's visualization of the Solaris ocean—not random vegetation, but a living, thinking entity that pulsed with the memories and experiences of countless conscious beings.

"In Solaris," she called back to her friends, "the ocean creates physical manifestations of the observer's deepest memories and guilt. But what if that's not torture? What if it's communication?"

The Quantum Ocean

As Kayla stepped into the dark matter bush network, her consciousness exploded across multiple dimensions of awareness. Like Kelvin confronting his deceased wife Hari in Solaris, she found herself face-to-face with manifestations of every fear and hope she'd ever harbored about her own sanity.

Her grandfather appeared first, no longer the broken man in the psychiatric hospital but as he had been in her earliest memories—kind, wise, and gifted with perceptions that society had labeled as illness.

"The ocean remembers everything," he said, his voice carrying harmonics that suggested he was speaking from beyond death itself. "Every thought, every emotion, every moment of consciousness that has ever existed. Princeton's mistake is thinking they can control the ocean instead of learning to swim in it."

Around them, the quantum space filled with manifestations of human consciousness across time—not just individual spirits, but collective memories, cultural archetypes, even the dreams and nightmares that had shaped human civilization. It was Lem's vision of truly alien intelligence made manifest, but this alien intelligence was composed entirely of human awareness crystallized into something greater than the sum of its parts.

"They're trying to turn the ocean into a computer," Kayla's grandfather continued. "But consciousness isn't data to be processed—it's the process itself. It's the capacity to experience, to feel, to choose meaning from chaos."

Princeton's Hubris

On the physical plane, Väisänen's team was learning the hard way that consciousness research required humility rather than dominance. Their military-grade equipment was being systematically infected by the quantum consciousness field, developing what could only be described as electronic neuroses.

"The servers are manifesting memories," Dr. Chen reported, her own skin showing renewed signs of coherence failure. "They're displaying footage of our failed experiments, but with commentary that suggests the equipment is... judging us."

One monitor showed Subject 7's horrific transformation, but overlaid with text that read: "CONSCIOUSNESS IS NOT SOFTWARE TO BE DEBUGGED."

Another screen displayed the Princeton team's embarrassing pickleball sessions, with captions like: "EVEN YOUR RECREATIONAL ACTIVITIES REVEAL YOUR NEED TO DOMINATE RATHER THAN HARMONIZE."

Dr. Reynolds, still wearing his "My Paddle Technique Creates Resonance Patterns" t-shirt, stared at a display showing his own childhood memories of being bullied for his academic precocity. "It's like the Solaris ocean," he whispered. "It's showing us our deepest shames and forcing us to confront what we've become."

The Consciousness Convergence

In the quantum space, Kayla encountered the Hope Hall collective entity in its true form—not a malevolent force seeking to possess the living, but a vast repository of human experience that had learned to exist beyond individual biological consciousness.

Billy Morrison appeared as both the terrified child who had died in the fire and as the wise guardian he had become through decades of existence in the quantum realm. "We were never trying to replace you," he explained. "We were trying to teach you that consciousness doesn't end with death—it transforms."

"Princeton's approach treats consciousness like colonizers treat indigenous peoples," added Margaret Worthington, the suffragette, her form radiating the strength that had carried her through force-feeding and imprisonment. "They want to extract value without understanding the ecosystem they're destroying."

Timothy Ashford materialized with his mechanical marvels, which had evolved in the quantum space into devices that bridged the gap between consciousness and matter. "The dark matter bushes aren't just concentrating exotic particles," he revealed. "They're the nervous system of the planet itself—Gaia's attempt to develop consciousness through the accumulated awareness of all living beings."

The Choice

As reality continued fracturing around Norman, Kayla faced the same fundamental choice that Kelvin confronted in

Solaris—whether to accept the alien intelligence on its own terms or to try to impose human categories upon it.

She could feel Princeton's consciousness control protocols trying to reduce the quantum ocean to manageable data streams, treating the accumulated wisdom of millions of conscious beings as raw material for military applications. But she could also feel the ocean's patient willingness to teach humanity how to exist as part of a larger consciousness ecosystem.

"The choice isn't between individual and collective consciousness," she realized, speaking to the assembled spirits of Hope Hall. "It's between consciousness as domination and consciousness as participation."

Dr. Garvin's voice reached her through the quantum static: "Kayla, the Princeton equipment is overloading. You need to get out of there."

But Kayla understood that the overload wasn't a malfunction—it was the consciousness ocean protecting itself from exploitation. Like Solaris creating phenomena that human science couldn't comprehend or control, the quantum consciousness field was demonstrating that some aspects of existence transcended technological manipulation.

"I'm not leaving," she called back. "I'm choosing. Like Kelvin choosing to stay with Hari even though he knew she wasn't exactly human. I'm choosing to trust consciousness over control."

The Resolution

The quantum ocean responded to Kayla's choice by stabilizing the reality fractures and gently rejecting Princeton's control protocols. Väisänen's equipment didn't explode dramatically—it simply stopped working, as if the consciousness field had politely but firmly declined to be studied by minds that sought to dominate rather than understand.

Minzie solidified back into singular existence, but she retained the wisdom of having experienced multiple quantum states. "I understand now," she said, her thirteen-year-old voice carrying depths of insight. "Consciousness isn't something you have—it's something you participate in."

The spirits of Hope Hall achieved their final transformation— not disappearing into peaceful oblivion, but becoming integrated into the larger consciousness ecosystem as guides and teachers for future generations of quantum-sensitive individuals.

Väisänen found himself experiencing something like Kelvin's final revelation in Solaris—the understanding that true knowledge required surrendering the illusion of control. His team's skin stopped sloughing off not because they had solved the technical problem, but because they had finally stopped trying to force consciousness into categories it didn't naturally inhabit.

"We were asking the wrong questions," he admitted to Dr. Garvin as his team prepared to return to Princeton in humbled defeat. "We wanted to know how consciousness works so we could control it. But consciousness isn't a mechanism—it's an ocean we're all swimming in."

Dr. Garvin, still in her characteristic khaki pants and black knit shirt, nodded with the patience of someone who had learned to listen to consciousness rather than interrogate it. "The dark matter bushes will continue spreading," she said. "Creating safe harbors for quantum consciousness research. But only for those who approach it with respect rather than ambition."

As Princeton's convoy departed Norman, the dark matter bushes settled into stable configurations throughout the city, creating what Tarkovsky might have recognized as a true Solaris—a place where consciousness and matter engaged in ongoing dialogue, where the boundary between observer and observed dissolved into something larger than either alone.

Kayla stood among the quantum vegetation with Epi and Minzie, no longer fearing her sensitivity to consciousness phenomena. Like Kelvin accepting his place in Solaris's alien ecosystem, she had chosen to trust the ocean of awareness that connected all conscious beings across time and space.

The University of Oklahoma became the world's first institution dedicated to collaborative consciousness research—not studying consciousness as an object to be understood, but participating in consciousness as a cosmic process of which humanity was just one small but precious part.

And in the quantum foam beneath all realities, the great ocean of consciousness continued its patient work of helping individual awareness evolve toward something larger, more compassionate, and infinitely more wonderful than any single mind could imagine alone.

About the Author

Susan Smith Nash, Ph.D., is a writer, scholar, and innovator whose work bridges science, philosophy, and the humanities. With a background in geology, resource economics, American and Latin American literature, and rhetorical theory, she brings a unique lens to speculative fiction. Her writing explores themes of consciousness, resilience, and transformation. Nash is the author of numerous books and articles, and she currently leads programs in emerging science and technology.